# THE TWISTED TALE OF SAFFRON SCHMIDT

C. J. LAURENCE

Copyright © 2019 C.J. Laurence
www.cjlauthor.com

All rights reserved.

First Edition

ISBN: 978-1-7109-1374-3

Cover Designer: Dark Imaginarium Art

No part of this book may be reproduced, scanned, or distributed in any printed or electronic form without permission. Please do not participate in or encourage piracy of copyrighted materials in violation of the author's rights. Thank you for respecting the hard work of this author.

This is a work of fiction. Names, characters, places, and incidents either are the product of the author's imagination or are used fictitiously, and any resemblance to locales, events, business establishments, or actual persons—living or dead—is entirely coincidental.

*For my wonderful friend, Elicia. I value you more than you know.*

CHAPTER ONE

Saffron slid her small palm over the smooth brown leather cover of her new book. When she opened it, she beamed with joy. Its crinkled, aged pages were thick and musty smelling. Each right-hand page harboured a beautiful hand drawn picture of the story being told in curly black handwriting on the left-hand page.

"Let's begin, children," Frau Hood said, standing at the front of the classroom. "Here is your history of our prosperous town..."

*Once upon a time, there lived a beautiful forest queen. A magnificent being so dainty and elegant, everything around her thrived with life. One day, a man from the city hiked through the abundant woods, curious what lovely sights he may find hidden inside to distract him from the ugliness of the modern world.*

*After hours of fighting with thick branches and losing sense of direction, Wilhelm Holtzmann finally pushed through the other side of the forest to set eyes upon a vast open plain. Lush green grass spread over the horizon, encircled by the woods completely.*

*Wilhelm fell in love instantly. He skipped across the long grass, laughing and thanking the universe for such splendour. Immediately he knew this was the place where he could escape the confines and mental struggles of a society he had come to hate. This was where he wanted to raise his family.*

*Mapping things out in his mind, Wilhelm started making plans for the home he would build here. Then he thought of his friends and other family members, realising that despite his hatred for the City, he couldn't live without seeing them.*

*"I'll invite them, too," he thought to himself. "There is more than enough room here for all of us."*

*And so, Wilhelm was soon imagining a village, an old-fashioned community where money was a foreign substance, and everyone pitched in to help survive—the way it should be.*

*Full of ideas and joy, Wilhelm turned to go home, only to be met with a pulsing green light blinding his view. As he tried to push forwards, the light became stronger, and as it burned brighter, started to hum with a low-pitched tremor.*

*Wilhelm, frightened, fell backwards, staring up at the paranormal phenomenon. The light lessened, and as it did, the shadow of a small human started to form in the centre of its presence. As Wilhelm took in the breath-taking sight before him, a soft, female voice spoke to him through his mind. Entranced by her gentle tones, Wilhelm could do nothing but listen.*

*"I can see your mind, human. I can feel your emotions; your pain, your hope, your need for freedom. My forest can provide you with what you seek, however, should you treat this place with anything but the utmost respect, you will be immediately removed from my domain. What you reap, you must sow, and there will be no death except those of natural causes."*

*Wilhelm nodded, hypnotised by the fairy floating in front of him. The light faded away, taking with it the exquisite forest spirit. Excited for his new adventure, Wilhelm immediately got to work, telling his friends and family of his marvellous idea. Within a few weeks, wooden frames turned into cosy homes, spread apart on the vast expanse of lush green grass. The towns folk decided to call their new home 'Sehrstadt' which loosely translated meant 'Very Town'. Their new home was very beautiful, very fruitful, and very giving. It was a place of very good things to come.*

*The fairy Queen lived for many, many years, deep inside the rich forest surrounding the village of Sehrstadt. However, after centuries of pouring her life essence into the wonderful woodland, the Queen died without an heir.*

*Within days, the forest started to die, no longer kept alive by the pure heartbeat of a worthy Queen. The Queen's confidantes summoned Wilhelm to the heart of forest and demanded he leave or provide the forest with a new Queen. Panicked and desperate to keep his blooming family in Sehrstadt, Wilhelm consulted with his closest family and friends.*

*It was decided, to repay the fairies for their generosity over the years, that they would indeed sacrifice one of their own to take on the role of being Queen. After deliberation with the fairies, it was revealed that they needed a young, innocent female whose pure essence could give the forest the heartbeat it needed to continue thriving. Desperate to keep his community together, Wilhelm said he would give them his own seventeen-year-old daughter, Adala.*

*However, to be deemed worthy enough of filling the empty throne, Adala would have to endure thirty days and thirty nights in the forest, surviving solely off the fruits offered to her by nature. Only if she survived this would she be crowned as the forest spirits new Queen.*

*Not wanting to scare Adala away from the monu-*

*mental task ahead, Wilhelm kept quiet about the mission she faced. Instead, he asked her to go into the forest to seek out a rare 'corpse' flower before the autumn equinox. It was needed because of its pungent smell similar to that of a rotting corpse.*

"We need it to keep the rodents away from the grain during winter," *he said to her, handing her a basket of water, bread, nuts, and berries.* "There is enough for a few days. You should be back before then."

*Adala, full of excitement to complete such an important task for her father, skipped out into the forest, her blue cotton dress swinging above her knees, and her red riding hood billowing out behind her.*

*The townsfolk held their breath for the next thirty days. When the browning leaves suddenly turned evergreen, birds started chirping morning songs once more, and the forest bustled again with energy, Sehrstadt realised that Adala had done the impossible—she had survived the forest and been deemed worthy of being their new Queen.*

*And so, in deep respect to pay thanks to Adala, every seventeen years, a young seventeen-year-old girl has been sent out into the forest to carry out the same journey that Adala did all those years ago. A stunning carved statue of Wilhelm's firstborn is situated in the middle of the forest and offerings are made to it by the chosen girl.*

*To say thanks for the ritual, Adala grants the chosen one an escape from the forest, letting them pass through and into the wide world beyond.*

"And that, my dear children, is the fantastical history of Sehrstadt," said Frau Hood. "Because of that, here we are today, living in this beautiful town, a perfect mix of old traditions with a touch of modern amenities. Does anyone have any questions?"

"What if the chosen one doesn't want to live away from Sehrstadt?" Saffron asked, frowning.

Frau Hood's round smiley face darkened with a thunderous look. "All children, when they reach that age in life, want to explore and see what lays beyond our borders." She clapped her hands together and then smiled at the rest of the class. "Now, children, let's—"

Saffron put her hand up and said, "But what if they really don't want to?"

"Saffron, look around you."

Frowning, Saffron took a hesitant glance around her at the rest of her class. A sea of young faces stared back at her, some blank, some scowling, some smiling.

"Eighty per cent of Sehrstadt's children go on to live in the City. In five years time, hardly any of your classmates will remain here," she replied, her tone of voice curt.

"What if it's the year of the Offering and there isn't a suitable girl?"

Frau Hood narrowed her eyes at the inquisitive young girl. "There is always a suitable child. Nothing happens by chance, Saffron, remember that."

"But—"

"That's enough for today, Saffron Schmidt."

Saffron closed her mouth and chewed over her teacher's words. What if there wasn't a suitable child for the Offering? Then what? What if the Chosen One didn't want to live in the City? Then what?

CHAPTER TWO

"How did you get on today, sweetie?" Saffron's mother, Anna, said as she walked through the door after school.

Saffron held up her book and frowned at her mother. "I got my book, but Frau Hood wouldn't answer my questions."

Anna blew a blonde curl out of her eyes as she kneaded the bread dough on the aged wooden pastry board. "What questions did you have? Maybe I can help."

Saffron dumped her new book down on the sturdy kitchen table. The resounding thud as the leather slapped against the solid oak surface made Anna jump. "What if the Chosen One doesn't want to go to the City? Does Adala make them leave?"

"I can honestly say, sweetheart, that hardly any

children want to stay here once they have the option to leave."

"But why? This is our home."

Anna sighed. "Most of the children have visited the City for several years beforehand. The sights, the smells, the busyness of it attracts them to want to know more." She lifted her head and gave her daughter a beaming smile. "You're thirteen now, Saffron. You'll soon be adventuring on the monthly supply trips. Then you will understand why no Chosen Ones have come back."

"What if there isn't a suitable child for the Offering? Then what?"

Sadness filled Anna's sky-blue eyes. "There is always a suitable child, sweetie."

"But what if, by some freak incident, there isn't?"

"Saffron, sweetie, you really do think about things too much."

Saffron sighed. "When is the next Offering? Four years?"

Anna nodded.

"What if all the children who will be seventeen that year have gone by then."

Anna gave a gentle laugh. "That won't happen, Saffron. Are you forgetting our most basic law?"

A lightbulb went off in Saffron's head. "No child under the age of eighteen shall leave Sehrstadt."

"Exactly," Anna said. "That's not just for your protection, that's for ours, too. Babies are being born every year, but should something happen where that doesn't happen, we can perhaps negotiate with the forest spirits to offer a different child."

"Why is it for our protection that we don't leave Sehrstadt until we're eighteen?"

"Because the City is an unforgiving modern monster. Who do you think would help someone who dresses like we do, has no money, and no sense of society? Money is a pivotal thing in the City, Saffron. Without money, you would starve to death, if you didn't die from thirst first. City people are too wrapped up in themselves to consider helping anyone who lives like we do. They judge you on your looks and how worthy you are of their time as a result." Anna let out a long sigh. "And the sad thing is, if you were any younger than that, going into the City alone, there are some very unsavoury characters out there who would exploit you in ways you can't even imagine."

Saffron looked down at her ankle length, full sleeved pink dress. "What's wrong with the way we dress? And what do you mean they would exploit us? How?"

Anna smiled as she reached for the bread tin. "You're a little too young to go into details of that with, Saffron." Anna looked at her daughter and gave her a warm smile. "I tell you what, I'll have a word with Herr Schulz and see if we can get you on the next supply trip. Then you can answer your own questions about the City."

"Really?" Saffron squealed and clapped her hands together. "Mama, that would be amazing." She rushed forwards and slipped her arms around her mother's soft waist, squeezing her tight.

"Don't thank me just yet, Saffron. Nothing has been agreed. Herr Schulz may deny the request."

"I know, I know, but I have a good feeling about this."

Anna pressed her lips together in a tight-lipped smile. "Let me finish this bread then, sweetie. Go and entertain yourself for a while."

Saffron gave a contented sigh, scooped her book up from the table, and ran into her small bedroom. Her single bed sat underneath a window, its crystal-clear glass taking up half of the back wall. Saffron could see her two sisters playing ball outside with their younger brother.

Jumping onto her wad of grey wool blankets, Saffron plumped up her pillow and settled back against the solid mahogany headboard with her Sehrstadt story book. Saffron opened up the first page, drinking in the colourful picture of the forest fairy on the right-hand page. The multiple shades of greens hypnotised her as she stared at the vivid art.

Page by page, Saffron read and re-read the story of Sehrstadt until every little detail of her town's history was engrained into her brain. Satisfied, and humming happily to herself, Saffron gently placed her new book on the large shelf above her bed, nestling it into place between all of her other books.

"Saffron!" Walter, her father, shouted her from the kitchen.

"Coming, Papa."

Running into the kitchen, overwhelmed by the tantalising smell of freshly baked bread, Saffron saw her father stood in the doorway. His clothes were covered in black marks, most likely soot or burns, and his face harboured grubby streaks of dirt and grime.

"Come and help me with the mare, please, Saffron."

Saffron rolled her eyes. "Hanna, Papa. She has a name."

Walter huffed as his daughter skipped towards him. "We've been through this, Saffron. Naming animals makes you emotionally attached. In the world we live in, it's best not to become attached. They serve a purpose. That is all."

"They deserve more than being treated as slaves,

Papa. We couldn't do half of the things we do without the animals."

"Exactly, Saffron. It's their job. Nothing more, nothing less. They are a necessity for us, not a privilege. We name pets, not workers."

Saffron frowned at her father. Deciding keeping quiet was the best option, mostly learned from previous experience, Saffron proceeded to help her father unharness their Belgian draught horse from their rickety old cart.

Henry, Hanna's three-year-old son, neighed to her from their shared pasture. He trotted up and down the fence line, his brown eyes bright and full of life at seeing his mother after a long day alone.

"How has your day been?" Walter asked his daughter.

"I got my book," Saffron said, then proceeded to explain how Frau Hood had refused to answer her questions. "Mama said that any child that goes to the City never wants to come back here. Is that true?"

Walter nodded and sighed. "Sadly, yes. The City, compared to here, is a bright, colourful world full of endless opportunities. We're all too easily forgotten out here with our simple way of life. We have nothing to offer compared to the City."

"But it's wonderful living here. It's so peaceful,

everything is so easy and relaxed. I don't understand why anyone would want to leave."

"Think of the City as like a bright shiny ring to a magpie. It can't resist, and neither can the children. It blinds them with opportunities and promises. Once they've been sucked in, it's impossible to see anything else."

"I want to be a blacksmith like you, Papa," Saffron said, sliding Hanna's bridle from her head. She held a headcollar in front of the chestnut mare's face, which she eagerly slid her head into.

"A forge is no place for a woman, Saffron. We've had this discussion before. Here, we live very simple, clear cut lives. Men do physical hard-working jobs, women mind the house and the children."

"But Frau Beck runs her own bakery."

"Yes, Saffron. A bakery—that's a woman's job. It's easy and allows for other chores to be carried out in the meantime. It fits around looking after children and the house."

Walter pushed the cart away, heading into the barn. Saffron clicked to Hanna and led her towards the lush green field with her eager son awaiting her return. As she trundled down the gentle slope towards the wooden gate, Saffron let her eyes drift to the forest beyond. Her imagination ran wild as she fantasised about the fairy Queen coming to see her, telling her she had been chosen to give the Offering but that she could return to Sehrstadt if she so desired.

"I think I would take you, Hanna," she said to the mare, stroking her neck. "It's been a while since you had a day off to go for a long ride. What do you think?"

Hanna nickered in response, pricking her ears forward at Henry.

Saffron opened the gate and let Hanna through. The mare waltzed in and allowed her son to snuffle through her mane before they indulged in a mutual scratching session of each other's backs.

Sighing in contentment, Saffron closed the gate and leaned on it, watching the two horses in blissful peace. Twilight insects started buzzing through the air and the humidity of the summer sun had lessened now sunset bathed Sehrstadt in a beautiful orange glow. A cool breeze slid through the forest, kissing Saffron's skin with such a light touch, she shivered.

With a growling stomach, Saffron headed indoors, grateful for another day in Sehrstadt.

CHAPTER THREE

"Good news, Saffron!" Anna said, bursting through her daughter's bedroom door a few mornings later. "Herr Schulz has approved you going on the next supply trip."

Saffron sprang upright, her blonde hair flying all over the place. "Really? Oh, Mama! Thank you so much!"

"Hurry," Anna said, shooing her daughter out of bed. "It's today and the cart leaves in thirty minutes."

Shrieking in delight, Saffron jumped out of bed and hurried to her wardrobe. Flicking through her various dresses, she pulled out her favourite—a sky blue knee length cotton dress. She grabbed her pair of black leather shoes and in less than ten minutes, burst into the kitchen, her freckled round face lit up in joy.

Anna took one look at her daughter and then

glanced at her husband, a silent message exchanging between the husband and wife.

"What?" Saffron said, noticing the look. "What's wrong?"

"Nothing, sweetie," Anna said, stepping forwards to hug her eldest child. "You just look so grown up." She fiddled with the two plaits Saffron had braided her blonde hair into. "I love your hair like this. You look so pretty."

Saffron looked at her father who gave a simple nod of his head. She knew her father was very much the strong, silent type. Never one to share too much emotion or pay many compliments, if any at all.

"They're waiting at the town hall," Anna said, handing Saffron a white riding hood. "This will help shield you from the sun. You're so pale and you know how easily you burn."

Saffron nodded and slipped the long white cloak over her shoulders, letting it cover her completely.

"Mama!"

Nikolas, Saffron's younger brother, screamed for his mother's attention. He was such a mama's boy and demanded all of her attention more or less all of the time. Anna rushed to his bedroom to fetch him before he shouted the house down.

"Help me harness the mare before you go, Saffron, please," said Walter, standing from the kitchen table.

He tossed her a warm crusty bread roll. "Don't forget your breakfast."

Saffron caught the small round bun and bit into it, loving the soft warmth that filled her mouth. "These are so good, Mama. I could live off these for a month."

Anna grinned as she wandered back into the kitchen, cradling the attention grabbing three-year-old on her hip. Walter ruffled Nikolas' hair before motioning for Saffron to head outside.

"I'll drag the cart out whilst you fetch the mare," Walter said, striding off towards the barn.

Saffron rushed down to the paddock, surveying the forest background beyond. A quiver of excitement ran up and down her spine as she revelled in the fact she would be adventuring through the thick trees in a matter of minutes.

Hanna stood waiting at the gate, more than used to the morning routine she had lived for the past sixteen years. Saffron led her up to the waiting cart, chatting to the placid horse excitedly about the day ahead of her.

As Saffron closed the last few strides towards the cart, Walter rushed forwards, snatching Hanna's lead rope from his daughter's hands.

"Stop delaying my day for the sake of your own silly fantasies," Walter said, his tone sharp and cutting.

"I can walk and talk, Papa," Saffron replied, giggling.

"The mare can't understand you, Saffron. Stop wasting your breath."

Saffron shook her head as she picked up Hanna's bridle. Glancing over her shoulder to make sure her father was otherwise distracted, Saffron placed a small piece of her warm bread roll over the cold metal bit she was about to slide into Hanna's mouth.

If her father caught her pandering to the horse's wants, he would lash her for sure. Saffron was more sympathetic to the fact that Hanna liked something warm to help her tolerate the coldness of the bit until it warmed to her mouth. It was a trick she'd learned from her friend's father who trained the community's animals.

Saffron buckled up the bridle in double quick time, smirking to herself at Hanna's twinkling eyes as she sucked on the piece of warm bread. Her father would just assume she was fiddling with the bit.

"Whatever ideals you hold in that head of yours, Saffron, get rid of them now. The City is nothing like you're going to expect."

Saffron pursed her lips. "Yes, Papa."

"Get on your way, before you miss the cart."

Not needing to be told twice, Saffron ran towards the town centre, past various different houses and families, all going about their morning routines.

In the very heart of Sehrstadt stood a large stone

fountain, its three simply decorated tiers cascading water in a peaceful stream. Several wooden benches were dotted around the focal point, enabling Sehrstadt's residents to sit and relax in the middle of their town. Situated all around the fountain, in a U-shaped formation, were all of the shops. Thirty-metre-wide passageways gave ample room for horses and carts to pass between the shops and the seating area in the middle.

At the apex of the U sat the town hall, its circular spire protruding several feet above the rooftops of the surrounding buildings. No exact religion existed in Sehrstadt, but the town hall was a communal place of many faces, including a place of worship for anyone who wished to indulge.

Saffron caught sight of the two draught horses attached to a huge wagon. Several adults were already sat in the open back, and a couple of older children too. Running faster, Saffron lifted her arm and waved.

"I'm here," she yelled.

One of the adults, Frau Mueller, smiled at her and moved up on the bench, patting the space beside her. Saffron slowed to a walk and made a beeline for the horses, taking a moment to say hello and give them a quick pat.

When Herr Wagner and Herr Bauer climbed up into the driver positions, Saffron scurried to the back, accepting a hand up from one of the older children to climb into the wagon. She had barely sat down before the horses were urged forwards, lurching the old wooden cart forwards sharply.

Saffron resisted the urge to squeal in excitement.

"You might want to pull your hood up, dear," Frau Mueller said, a warm smile playing out on her thin lips. "You don't want to get sun stroke." She patted the top of her head and flicked up her own hood on her white riding cloak.

"Thanks," Saffron said, pulling her hood over her head.

Looking behind her, Saffron soaked in the sight of her beloved birthplace. Whilst she felt apprehensive and excited for experiencing the City for the first time, she still couldn't fathom how anyone could want to leave such a serene town.

She spotted her father trotting Hanna towards his forge on the outskirts of the town. Because of the size of his workshop and the dangerousness of his activities inside, the forge sat back from the main town square, a good quarter of a mile away to stop any young, curious minds from accidentally wandering in.

Saffron scanned the treeline, her mind drifting back to the new book sat on her bookshelf. As she looked at the dense forest surrounding her town, she once again envisioned a dainty green fairy appearing before her, telling her things no one else could hear. She wondered how Wilhelm must have felt, being at the epicentre of something so amazing and paranormal.

All of a sudden, Saffron's world darkened, making her heart jump into her mouth. She whirled around to see the wagon had entered the forest. Glancing ahead, she could see a well-worn trail stretching straight in front of them, its sandy yellow base a stark contrast to the deep greens and browns of the forest surrounding it.

"You're going to love the City," said Mia Fischer.

Saffron turned her attention to the sixteen-year-old brunette. "What's it like?"

"It's amazing," Mia replied, her brown eyes lighting up with joy. "Everything is so busy, so bright and colourful, there's so much going on. It's impossible to take it all in at once. The buildings, the people, the cars—"

"Cars?"

Mia grinned. "Horses are old technology to them. They're nothing more than pets now. They have these machines, called cars, that they drive to get them places. They go really fast and they're really strange looking but in a really cool way. You'll learn about them in class this year."

Saffron felt an ache setting into her cheeks from

her wide, excited grin. "I can't wait. Can you show me around?"

"Sure. I mean, only as much as we're allowed. We go to specific places and then come straight back. We won't be there much more than an hour or two."

Saffron nodded.

The rhythmic beat of the trotting horses took them through the deepest parts of the forest. It took Saffron several minutes to realise that the thud-thud from the draught horses hooves was the only sound around them.

Frowning, she turned to Mia and said, "Why can't I hear any birds? Or anything for that matter?"

Mia's eyes widened and she quickly glanced at Frau Mueller. Her mouth opened, but she said nothing.

"Wildlife doesn't come this close to the City trails," Frau Mueller replied. "The forest spirits give them borders to keep within, to keep them safe."

"Why?"

"Because the City people are cruel, Saffron. That's why the forest spirits protect our borders so much. City people are like a tidal wave of destruction and death. They don't appreciate nature in all its finest beauty. All they see is money. If they ever came across our lands, they would wipe out our town in a matter of days and the forest with it."

Saffron gasped. "And do what with it?"

"Either build some of their ugly, modern buildings or compete against each other for rights to the land. Land like ours is prime for so many things, it would be worth a fortune to them."

"But they must know where we come from?" Saffron motioned over her clothes and at the cart. "They must know something about our town, surely?"

Frau Mueller sighed. "They have tried many times to follow us back, even gone so far as putting some of their little gadgets on our cart to track our movements, but the forest spirits always protect us, so their efforts have always failed."

Saffron's heart started beating harder, pumping spurts of adrenaline into her bloodstream. "So we really do owe everything to Adala?"

Frau Mueller nodded, her angular face lighting up with happiness. "She protects us well with her powers and her community of fairies."

"When is the next Offering again?"

"Four years."

Saffron's heart somersaulted. "I'll be seventeen in four years..."

Mia reached forwards and wrapped her small hand around Saffron's forearm. "You're so lucky! At least you have a chance of being chosen. I'll be twenty by then. I love the City, but I don't want to live in it. I'm going to be nothing more than a permanent resident of Sehrstadt."

"Not that there's anything wrong with that," said Frau Mueller. "We all have a purpose, a role to play, in order to keep our community thriving. Everything happens for a reason, Mia. Sometimes it just takes a while for the reason to make itself known."

Mia nodded and looked down at the battered wooden floor of the wagon. Saffron smiled at Frau Mueller and continued to gaze around her, soaking in the dense trees empty of anything but wood and dirt.

The horses suddenly jolted to a stop, neighing and stamping their feet. The wagon lurched forwards, sending all the passengers flying from their seats. Herr Wagner cracked his whip over the horse's rumps as Herr Bauer shouted at them to move on. Both refused to move, fidgeting on the spot and snorting in fear.

A burst of adrenaline pulsed through Saffron's body. Before she knew what she was doing, she jumped down from the back of the wagon and rushed to the horses.

"Saffron Schmidt!" yelled Herr Wagner. "What do you think you're doing? Get back in the wagon immediately!"

Frau Mueller and Mia both shouted for her to return but Saffron stood her ground, more focused on calming the agitated horses.

"Shhhh," she said, sliding her hand along the thick neck of the grey stallion who had fathered Henry. "Easy, boy."

Scanning the environment around her, Saffron tried to pinpoint something in the treeline that seemed off, that might be the cause of freaking the horses out. Not seeing anything obvious, she stepped out in front of the horses, walking the path they were refusing to continue down.

"Saffron Schmidt!" Herr Wagner shouted, his voice trembling. "Return to this wagon immediately or I will report you to Herr Schulz."

Saffron ignored him. The hairs on the back of her neck stood up, a wave of goosebumps coating her body from head to toe. In the blink of an eye, all of her senses seemed to be on high alert. Her eyes darted from tree to tree, her ears concentrated on every little noise, and her nose tried to pick out any scent different to that of the fresh forest.

Step by step, Saffron soon found herself several hundred yards in front of the horses. Her fellow townsfolk had long since fell into silence, leaving the brave young girl alone to face whatever was spooking the horses.

Out of nowhere, a violent gust of ice-cold wind blew through the forest, nearly knocking Saffron off her feet.

*"Saffffronnnn..."*

Saffron froze, her limbs paralysed with fear. She fought an internal war to reason with herself as to what she had just heard. Convincing herself it was nothing more than the rustle of the branches and leaves, and her mind playing tricks on her, she bolted back to the horses, her heart pounding against her ribs.

Looking at the adults sat on the wagon, each one of them had paled to a sickly white colour. The wind disappeared as quickly as it had appeared, leaving the small group in utter shock for a good minute or more.

The horses calmed, finally standing still and chomping on their bits as they awaited their next instruction. Saffron snapped out of her daze and rushed to the back of the cart. She reached a hand up, and when no hand came to offer her help, she shouted, "Mia!"

Mia jumped, the sound of her name breaking whatever spell had been cast over her. "Sorry," she said, smiling. "Lost in my own daydreams there."

Saffron scrambled up into the back of the wagon and took her seat next to Frau Mueller. "Did you hear that?" Saffron asked.

"What's that, dear?" Frau Mueller replied.

"The wind...it said my name..."

"Oh, don't be silly," Frau Mueller said, clapping

her hands together. "The way the trees rustle does funny things to the mind."

The horses sprang into an active trot, pulling everyone back into reality. Silence fell over the startled residents as they headed towards the bright lights of BlauPferd.

CHAPTER FOUR

They left the forest and meandered along small and twisty hard grey lanes. Saffron was amazed by the solid surface that wasn't mud or dirt.

"What is that?" she asked, pointing at the country road they were trotting along.

"Tarmac," Frau Mueller said. "They dig up the land and lay this tarmac for their cars to drive on. They're called roads, but these are very small ones."

Saffron was both sad and surprised. She couldn't believe that people could scar Mother Nature to such an extent, but she was also taken aback by what the City people could do with machines and technology.

The winding tight roads merged into a large spaghetti network of huge, fast vehicles. Saffron stared at all the vehicles, mesmerised by them and their passengers inside. She couldn't wait to learn about the City in class.

Their wagon stayed straight, heading down an open highway right into the heart of a heaving metropolis. People stopped and stared as the horses and cart trundled along the hectic roads, holding up angry, frustrated citizens, all commanded by time. Whilst the City people were used to these monthly visits, it didn't make them any more patient or welcoming when their daily routines were interrupted.

Several cars sped by, loud ear-piercing noises blaring from them.

"What was that?" Saffron said, rubbing her ears.

"Horns," Frau Mueller said. "Now you've got your Sehrstadt book, you'll be learning about City life this term with Frau Hood. She will explain all the terminology, technology, and everything else."

Saffron couldn't help but gawp at everything around her. She felt like a toddler being introduced to a mountain of toys for the first time. Soaking in as much as she could, she missed when the wagon came to a stand still in the middle of a bustling city centre.

"Come on," Mia said, tugging at Saffron's arm.

Saffron realised they'd stopped and said, "How many shops do they need?"

Mia grinned. "They have two or three, sometimes even more, that sell the same things. It's bizarre."

Saffron jumped down from the cart and allowed Mia to take her along the smoothly paved streets. Some people bumped into her, too busy going about their day to worry about the strangely dressed young girls. Others gave them both scornful looks, disgusted at their choice of clothes.

"I'm going to show you the library," Mia said. "You'll love it."

Glancing back at the horses and cart, Saffron tried to get her bearings as Mia led her down past a red brick building with a picture of a black horse on a green background over the big front doors.

"It's a bank," Mia said. "It's where the City people keep their money."

"But how do they know whose is whose? Do they all share it?"

Mia giggled. "No. It's much more complicated than that. You'll learn about it soon enough."

The street alongside the bank was very quiet, barely half a dozen people walking down it, a stark contrast to the crowded main street a mere few feet back. Opposite the bank, a huge white wall of another building cast the side street into shadows, a few tables scattered along its walls, contained within a thick red velvet rope.

"It's a pub," Mia explained. "A public house. Like our bar but much bigger."

Saffron nodded, nearly tripping over as she tipped her head back taking in the huge height of the white pub.

They walked for several hundred yards, the street bearing a sharp left. To the right was a tall grey wall, its old bricks cracked and crumbling. To the left was the red wall that served as the back of the bank. Straight in front of them sat a glass fronted building, shelves and shelves of books already visible through its windows.

Saffron gasped. "Wow."

"I thought you'd like it. There are thousands of books in here. They don't let us take them away, but they let us read them until we have to leave."

Mia led Saffron inside the bland building and headed up the set of stairs straight in front of them. Saffron inhaled the sweet scent of books, the familiar smell easing a sense of calm over her. The magnolia coloured walls were barely visible amongst the hundreds of shelves and bookcases spread all around. A glass waist height barrier lined the edge of the upper level, allowing Saffron to peer down at the ground floor below.

"All the non-fiction is down there," Mia said. "Up here is all the fiction. There's so many good books in here, Saffron."

Saffron couldn't help but feel slightly disappointed. Taking in the plain brown carpet, the boring white walls, and the lacklustre books shelves, everything looked so...unremarkable. Nothing seemed to have character or life to it, no essence of being, it just *was*. The only colourful thing about this place was the books and their vivid covers. After all the hype she'd grown up hearing about how colourful and full of life the City was, she had expected her first experience of a City building to be something more.

Pushing her father's last words to the back of her mind, Saffron refused to admit he was right. This building was one of many. They wouldn't all be like this, surely?

Mia dragged Saffron up and down several rows of bookshelves. "Here," she said, thrusting a blue book into Saffron's hands. "This is book one of a series. It's fantastic."

Saffron stared at the bright blue cover, its edges bordered with black roses and thorny leaves. A pair of startling orange eyes glared back at Saffron, giving her an eerie feeling.

"Night World," she said. "Secret Vampire." She glanced up at Mia. "Really?"

"Read it. Trust me, you'll love it."

Before Saffron could even turn the book over to read the blurb, Mia was pulling her towards the back of the building. They came across a few wooden looking tables, most of which were unoccupied.

Saffron sat down on one of the hard chairs and ran her hand over the shiny table surface. "I'm confused," she said, frowning. "It looks like wood, but it doesn't feel like wood."

Mia grinned. "You've got so much to learn." She waved a book at Saffron—Vampire Academy—and said, "Get reading, quick. We haven't got much time."

"Have you got an obsession with vampires or something?" Saffron asked, giggling.

"Read that," Mia replied, nodding at Saffron's book. "Then tell me you're not obsessed."

Mia placed her gold pocket watch on the table so she could keep an eye on the time. They had an hour before they needed to return to the cart. The two girls fell into silence, both devouring their books as the minutes ticked by.

Saffron immediately fell in love with James and Poppy, the two main characters in the book Mia had given her. Halfway through the chapter where Poppy discovered James' secret, Mia jumped up, sucking in a deep breath.

"We're late!" she said, scraping the chair back across the carpet. "Come on, Saffron. Quick!"

"But I'm halfway through the best bit," Saffron said, protesting.

"It'll be here next time we come. You can finish it then."

"But what if it's not?"

"It will be," Mia said, dragging her friend back to the shelves to put the books away.

"You can borrow them if you like."

The soft male voice startled both of the girls, freezing them to the spot. Saffron turned around to see a handsome young man with skin the colour of chocolate looking at them. She gasped. Mia dug her fingernails into Saffron's arm, a distinct warning to shut up.

"Really?" Mia asked. "That would be so kind."

"Sure. Just come downstairs with me and we can fill the forms out."

Mia sighed. "We haven't got time. We're late getting back already."

The man pursed his lips and folded his arms over his chest. "Ok. You twisted my arm. I trust you. I've seen you in here every month for the past year. Just make sure your friend brings hers back too."

"Thank you so much!" Mia said, her eyes shining with joy. "We won't let you down."

Mia shook Saffron's arm. "Thank you," Saffron said, her voice barely a whisper.

The two girls ran outside, their new prizes tucked into their chests as they headed for their cart. Frau Mueller was in the back of the wagon, scanning the busy crowd for the girls. When she saw them both, she scowled, deep frowns creasing her forehead.

"You girls," she said, helping them both up into the cart. "You've kept us waiting for nearly ten minutes."

"Sorry," Mia said. "We got carried away reading." She held her book up and grinned wildly. "The man in the library said we could keep them until we come back again."

Frau Mueller glanced behind her quickly. "Shhhh," she said. "And hide those things, quickly. Before they get taken off you."

Saffron frowned. "Why?"

"We're not supposed to trust City people under any circumstances."

"But we come here for supplies?"

"Yes...from previous Offerings who have made a life here."

Saffron's eyes lit up like a Christmas tree. "You mean we still have contact with them? Can I meet one?"

"Possibly next time. Now quickly, hide that book."

Saffron hid it underneath her white riding cloak, then turned to Mia. "That man...the colour of his skin..."

"Yes," Mia said. "There are people in the world who have different coloured skin to us, but we have to be very careful what we say."

"Why?"

"It's political, very political. One of the many cons of living in the City. We are known as 'white'."

"And what would he be called?"

"A person of colour."

"Why is it so political?"

"You'll learn about it this year, Saffron. Honestly, it's really sad. People like him have been betrayed in so many ways. It's one of the reasons I want to stay in Sehrstadt. The City is like a beautiful rose—so pretty but prickly underneath."

Saffron frowned. "But his eyes, they were so big and brown, I've never seen anything so captivating in all my life. His skin looked so smooth and silky, it reminded me of Mama's coffee."

"I think you've got your first crush," Mia said, teasing Saffron.

"No," Saffron said, sharply. "I'm just admiring his natural beauty."

Mia giggled all the way back home. Saffron was itching to continue reading her book. Thoughts of the librarian continued to creep into her mind, her stomach fluttering whenever she pictured his face or thought about the deep husk to his voice.

When she arrived home, Saffron found her house empty. It was still too early for her father to be back from work. Her mother and her younger siblings were also not home. Saffron shrugged her shoulders, delighted to have some time to herself. Not needing any further encouragement, Saffron immersed herself back into the world of James and Poppy.

CHAPTER FIVE

Saffron devoured her book before her mother returned home with her rowdy brother and sisters in tow. Feeling on cloud nine at the heart-warming story she'd just read, Saffron couldn't wait for the next supply trip so she could continue with the next book in the series.

"How was your day?" Anna asked later on, as Saffron helped her prepare a beef stew.

"Fantastic, Mama! Thank you so much for getting me onto the supply trip. I can't wait for the next one."

Anna gave her a small smile but said nothing else on the matter.

Saffron hummed to herself as she stirred the massive pot of meat and vegetables, lost in daydreams of young love and optimism. After she had eaten and helped her mother clean up, Saffron returned to her bedroom and began to read her book all over again. She read until her eyelids became too heavy to keep open.

Falling into a deep sleep, Saffron soon found herself lost in a world of darkness...

*Saffron tiptoed through the forest. An eerie silence enveloped her, pulling her into the shadows of the ancient trees. Nothing moved. Not even a leaf stirred in the dense woods surrounding her. The only movement was from her, and as quiet as she may be, being in such deathly silence meant any movement screamed as loud as a wailing banshee.*

*The hairs on the back of her neck stood up. A chill covered her body, making her shudder violently. Saffron stopped dead in her tracks. Every sense heightened twenty levels. As she slowly surveyed the black world around her, trying in vain to see anything that might be out of place, a gust of wind burst through the trees, shaking their branches.*

*"Safffronnnnnn....."*

*She froze. The wind blew harder, knocking her into the tree behind her. Her shoulder crunched against the rough bark, a jolt of pain shooting through her bones.*

*"Safffffronnnn....."*

*Whirling around, her eyes wide with fear, Saffron could see nothing. Nothing but darkness. Not even a sliver of moonlight penetrated the thick canopy of treetops all around her. Putting her hands out in front of her, Saffron tentatively felt her way forwards, one step at a time.*

*A flicker of candlelight lit up in the middle of the abyss, not more than a few metres away. Saffron stifled a cry of joy and rushed towards it, still feeling her way with her hands. Several feet away, the wind died down, replaced instead by a gentle warm breeze that came in steady drafts.*

*Saffron revelled in the heat cloaking her, momentarily closing her eyes in a brief moment of pleasure. When she opened them, the candlelight was no more than an arm's length away. Not giving any thought to what the light could be, or how it was suspended in midair, Saffron blindly made a grab for it.*

*When her hands settled around the thick wax candle, Saffron dared to whisper, "Yes!" in victory. But as she tugged it towards her, it did not move. Saffron pulled harder, wanting the heat giving light closer to her. The candle did not move.*

*Warm puffs of air blew on her face, billowing her hair out behind her shoulders in a sunshine yellow stream. Her eyes watering from the pressure, Saffron moved her face, trying to find some relief from the air pressure. She tilted her face up and became instantly paralysed with fear.*

*Two huge brown eyes stared back at her, separated by thick grey fur. Saffron screamed, her throat raw with the sheer panic erupting from her voice box...*

Startling herself awake, Saffron sat bolt upright, sweat pouring from her body. Streaks of moonlight fell through her window, highlighting her bed. Her pulse racing and her head swimming from the stark reality of her nightmare, Saffron threw her covers off and padded into the kitchen for a drink of water.

As she lifted the glass to her lips, she realised her hands were shaking when she spilled water down her nightdress. Trying to push the vivid dream to the back of her mind, Saffron settled back into her bed, pulling the covers up tight to her chin.

No matter how hard she tried, she could not go back to sleep.

---

"Morning, sweetheart," Anna said, ambling into the kitchen the next morning. "Up early?"

Saffron nodded as she removed another batch of freshly baked rolls from the oven. "Thought I'd save you a job and cook breakfast."

"Thanks, Saffron," her mother replied, taking a seat at the table. "I really appreciate it. Did you sleep well?"

Saffron immediately stiffened, her shoulders and back visibly tense. "I had a bit of an odd dream."

"Oh?"

Pouring some orange juice into a glass, Saffron took a seat opposite her mother and grabbed one of the warm crusty rolls. Slicing it open, she allowed all the steam to escape before smothering the insides in a thick layer of butter.

"Do you want to talk about it?" Anna said.

Saffron took a bite of her food, satisfying her stomach for a brief second. After indulging her mother in the specific details of her nightmare, Saffron felt like a weight had been lifted from her shoulders.

"I'm sure it means nothing, sweetheart. Did anything happen in the City to warrant such a dream?"

Deciding to keep the secret of her book to herself, Saffron shook her head. "No. Nothing really remarkable happened at all."

"Not even on the journey in?"

Halfway to her mouth with her roll, Saffron froze. She lifted her eyes to meet her mother's, shock and uncertainty swirling through her mind. Did her mother know? Was this a test? Should she skip over the drama or admit to it?

"No, Mama," Saffron said, filling her mouth with her breakfast.

Anna nodded once but said nothing else on the matter. Her blue eyes clouded over with resignation and in that moment, Saffron knew that her mother knew, and worst of all, her mother knew she had just been lied to.

Guilt churned over and over in Saffron's stomach, curdling with distaste the longer the silence dragged on. After a minute or so, Saffron couldn't bear it any longer.

"Actually, thinking about it, something did happen."

Anna raised her eyebrows, her eyes lighting up with joy. "Really? What happened?"

Saffron took a deep breath then explained what happened with the horses on the trail. When she finished, she looked at her mother, expecting some wise words or something inspiring.

"I'm sure it was all in your mind, dear."

"But the adults all heard it, too."

"Have you heard of *folie à plusieurs?*"

Saffron frowned. "Err...no."

"It's basically group psychosis. So when one person experiences something, those around that person also start to believe they're experiencing the same thing."

Saffron's heart plummeted. "You think we were all hallucinating?"

"I'm just saying it's an option, Saffron. No one has ever reported anything odd happening on the trails. I'm sure you were just a little frightened and excited with it being your first trip out and your brain tried to make sense of it all but ended up in a bit of a muddle. It's nothing to be ashamed of."

Faking a smile, Saffron said, "I'm sure you're right, Mama."

"What are your plans for today?"

"The horse's paddock needs cleaning and Henry needs to start some basic training."

"Herr Schäfer is booked to start training him in a few weeks time."

"I can do something before then, make it easier for him when he does start."

"Saffron," Anna said, leaning forwards and placing her hand over her daughter's. "Training animals is not a woman's job. Leave the men to it. Sometimes the animals need a firm hand."

Saffron's heart skipped a beat. "What do you mean 'a firm hand'?"

"The general energy of a woman is much calmer and weaker than that of a man's. With a spirited young horse like Henry, he needs a dominating strong presence to show him the way."

"I don't like this, Mama," Saffron said, scraping her chair across the floor and standing up. "Everything in this town is either male or female. Why can't a woman do a man's job and a man do a woman's job?"

"Saffron, sweetie—"

"No, Mama. Don't 'sweetie' me. I thought Wilhelm created this whole town to give us a sense of life at its simplest form, to allow us to enjoy life and be able to do what we want to do."

Anna jerked her head back, shocked by her daughter's sudden outburst. It suddenly struck her that Saffron was now a teenage girl, prone to mood swings, hormone changes, and given her enquiring mind, a ticking time bomb to a whole lot of trouble if mismanaged.

"You're right, Saffron, that is why Wilhelm created this place. However, in order to live so simply and easy, jobs had to be divided between men and women. Otherwise we're living in no different way than those in the City."

"Except the cars, the clothes, the money, the technology—"

"Saffron, things are the way they are here for a reason. It works. Upsetting the balance is going to achieve nothing."

"Ok, fine. I get it—men do the hard, physical labours, women play house and have children.

Answer me this—why has no boy ever gone into the forest as an Offering? Why is it all girls? Men hunt to put the meat on our tables, because that's a man's job, right?"

Anna nodded.

"So why is the Offering only for girls? Why is it good enough to send one of us out into the forest then, but not at any other point?"

"Because the forest has a Queen, Saffron. It needs a female essence to thrive off. Women are more in touch with their emotions than men. It would be inappropriate to pay respects to the Queen with a boy rather than a girl. Why do you think we refer to Mother Nature as exactly that rather than Father Nature?"

Saffron shrugged her shoulders. "I guess because it's natural for a woman to be more nurturing."

"Exactly. And that's what this forest needs—an empathetic, nurturing soul to be its leader."

Letting out a big sigh, Saffron resigned herself to the fact that as long as she lived in Sehrstadt, her hopes and dreams would never be truly lived. Now she began to understand why eighty percent of the town's children skipped out to the City.

"Is Papa still sleeping?"

Anna nodded. "Why?"

"I know Sunday's are usually Hanna's day off, but I

would like to take her for a ride around the outskirts of the forest."

Anna raised an eyebrow. "As long as you don't go into the forest, Saffron. I think Hanna would like that though. It's been a while since she's done anything but pull that cart."

Saffron smiled at her mother. She sidestepped around the table, walked to her mother's side, and bent down to kiss her cheek. "I'm sorry I got so worked up. It's just really frustrating at times."

"It's ok, poppet," Anna replied, lifting a hand to her daughter's cheek. "I understand, I really do."

Rushing out into the early morning sun, Saffron couldn't wait for the day's adventure ahead of her.

CHAPTER SIX

It didn't take Saffron long to tack Hanna up. When the mare saw her saddle being plonked on the gate, she pricked her ears up and nickered to Saffron. Henry raised his head from the lush green grass, a tuft of long grass dangling out of his mouth.

"Your turn soon, Henry," Saffron called to him, giggling at his gormless appearance.

She led Hanna out of the gate, closed it, then climbed it, using it as a mounting block to reach the stirrups dangling halfway down Hanna's side. Hanna, more than used to Saffron's improvising the gate for a mounting block, sidled up against it so Saffron didn't have to reach out too far with her leg.

Safely seated in the saddle, Saffron clucked at Hanna, urging her forwards into a leisurely walk. Hanna had been voice trained as a two-year-old. With her main job being that of a carthorse, voice aids were much more useful to Walter than anything else. On the odd occasion Saffron decided to ride her, it made her life much easier as her legs barely reached past the saddle flaps, most of their length being taken up by the mare's broad back.

As they meandered out towards the forest, Saffron took a moment to enjoy the view of her town from horseback. It fascinated her how places could look so different from a change of perspective. Seeing the town on foot was very different to seeing it from the supply trip wagon and different again seeing it from Hanna's muscly back.

Sehrstadt was situated deep within the northern territory of The Black Forest. The Black Forest itself was over six thousand square kilometres of mysterious towns and villages, all lost in their own timeframe of human history. The area that Sehrstadt had grown on was a two-thousand-acre jagged circle of fertile land, surrounded by dense woodland. With Adala protecting the odd shaped patch of forest, Saffron found herself wondering if the other towns within the mountainous range even knew Sehrstadt existed.

Looking up, Saffron saw nothing but a clear blue sky, not a wisp of a cloud in sight. The sun was slowly rising high above the treeline, beaming its warm rays down to earth. Saffron took the reins in one hand, lazily resting her free hand on her thigh as she gently rocked back and forth with Hanna's ambling walk.

Being a Sunday, not many people were up and about before ten a.m., enjoying their day of rest fully. Saffron's body clock always woke her at dawn. Occasionally she indulged in laying in her bed, enjoying the soft warmth it provided. Today, however, was one of those days where she wanted to be up and revelling in the beauty of the day.

Saffron glanced over her shoulder, making sure her mother wasn't stood watching her. Satisfied she'd been left to her own devices, she pushed Hanna on towards the treeline, intent on wandering inside the forest, just a few steps. Waltzing through the trees a few feet within the treeline wouldn't cause any more damage than if she kept to the outer edge of it. After all, what difference did a few feet make?

As the forest came closer, Saffron's heart started to pound. She knew she was doing something wrong, yet she couldn't help herself. The forest intrigued her, and she wanted to explore. Rebelling against the rules she'd known since she was old enough to walk made Saffron's mind go wild with potential consequences if she got caught. She'd never known anyone to be punished for going against the rules because nobody ever had, as far as she knew.

The trees beckoned her like a moth to a flame.

Nothing stirred, not one bird chirped. Saffron frowned. She was well within the borders of the City trails here, yet still no animals seemed to be around such a vibrant forest.

Saffron sucked in a deep breath as Hanna marched into the treeline. Reminding herself that if there was any danger, Hanna would refuse to move, Saffron found her confidence growing with each stride the big mare took.

A hazy mist hovered between the trees, the early morning sun warming the overnight dew on the ground. Saffron dared to venture further in than she originally intended. Before she knew it, the outer edge of the forest was metres behind her.

Her pulse quickened. Excitement and adrenaline coursed through her veins. The reality that she was doing something forbidden never left the forefront of her mind. Guiding Hanna to the left, Saffron took a gentle sweeping curve around, cutting off her forwards progression into the depths of the unknown. Estimating she was roughly thirty metres inside the treeline, Saffron realised no one would be able to see her unless they were really looking for her.

"Perfect," she said to Hanna. "Means we can explore at our own leisure."

Hanna plodded on, her ears flicking back and forth as she listened to Saffron's ramblings.

Saffron surveyed the landscape around her, not entirely sure what she was looking for but yet, still looking for something. Anything. Anything that might hint to something more, something about Adala and the forest spirits.

The moss-covered ground was undisturbed, no signs of animal tracks or even her own people having been through here recently. Saffron frowned. A hunt had gone out just yesterday. She was certain they'd come this way.

"Probably further on," she said out loud, trying to explain away the lack of evidence. "Or deeper in."

They strolled along, horse and rider, in comfortable silence for several minutes. As much as she tried, Saffron couldn't ignore the fact that no living creature seemed to be out here or had left any trace of ever being here. Where was all the wildlife?

Hanna came to an abrupt halt, jolting Saffron forwards in the saddle. Immediately, Saffron went on high alert. She twisted around in the saddle, her head spinning wildly from side to side as she scanned the woods around her. The silence that had accompanied her this far, suddenly seemed to gain a whole new degree of quiet. A distinct chill settled in the air, making Saffron shiver.

Memories from yesterday stormed back to the front of her mind, leaving her anticipating another eerie gust of wind that somehow knew her name. She tensed up, bracing herself for the violent burst of air, but after several minutes, she realised nothing was coming.

Letting out a small sigh of relief, Saffron ordered Hanna forwards, but the mare refused to move. She didn't fuss, stomp her feet, or even neigh in fear, she just simply refused to walk forwards. Frustrated, Saffron let out a shout of exasperation. She couldn't dismount and lead her forwards because she'd never be able to mount the huge mare from the floor.

Saffron leaned forwards, looking down over Hanna's shoulder at the forest floor, checking for any obvious obstructions. Content there was nothing to the left, she switched sides and checked over the mare's right shoulder.

That's when she spotted it.

Not at first with a quick sweeping glance, but after a few seconds, when she roved her eyes slowly over the green earth in front of her.

A paw print.

Saffron's heart stopped dead. Suspended over Hanna's shoulder, looking down at the ground, she suddenly felt very vulnerable and that she was somewhere she really shouldn't be.

The single track a mere few inches in front of Hanna's right hoof gave Saffron the chills. It was huge. If Hanna put her dinner-plate sized foot in the print, it would barely cover half of it. Above the four pad marks were four claw marks, each one sliced into the earth.

"What is that?" she whispered. "A wolf? A cat?"

Her inquisitive mind overtook her pounding heart, making her forget her fears temporarily. The ground trembled beneath her. Sitting bolt upright, Saffron cast her eye through the trees around her. The trembling turned into a low rumble.

Hanna stepped backwards, shaking her head. Fear poured into Saffron's body, springing her into action. She turned Hanna left, facing her back towards the treeline and the safety of Sehrstadt beyond.

Except the treeline she'd glanced at moments ago was no longer there. Saffron was surrounded by nothing but a thick copse of trees, every single one looking the same. She whirled around, almost falling from the saddle as panic consumed every last part of her.

Then, as if someone had flicked a switch, everything went black. Terror climbed through Saffron's veins like ivy, claiming her inch by inch in nothing but a cold, sweaty coat of dread. She'd never seen such darkness. She couldn't even see the end of her nose. It's looming presence felt almost physical, as if someone had thrown a sheet of black velvet over her face.

She tried to breathe, to give herself room to think logically, but the horror building inside her shattered any sense of logic and rationalisation. Realising she was way out of her depth, Saffron acted on instinct in such an overwhelming situation—she squeezed her eyes shut and held her breath, hoping it would all go away.

Seconds ticked by.

Willing herself to find the courage to open one eye, Saffron dared to take a peek. Bright sunlight streamed into her vision along with the treeline and Sehrstadt beyond. Needing no further encouragement, she kicked Hanna and yelled, "Canter!" aiming for the blissful relief of her home.

Hanna leapt into action, her lolloping strides thundering across the forest floor. In a matter of seconds, horse and rider burst from the treeline like a bullet from a gun. Hanna kept pace, homed in on her target of her son and her lush green paddock. Saffron was focused on nothing but her house.

Even as Hanna put distance between them and the forest, Saffron couldn't resist a glance behind her. Something was happening in that forest, something dark, something that definitely wasn't fairies and all things nice.

At that moment, Saffron knew that wouldn't be her last trip into the mysterious woods surrounding her home.

CHAPTER SEVEN

Saffron told no one about her experience in the forest with Hanna. As the days passed her by, Saffron couldn't help but spend more and more time staring into the leafy depths that surrounded her home. She'd heard the expression curiosity killed the cat, and despite her head screaming nothing but danger at her, Saffron still had an incurable desire to explore further inside the extensive woodland.

The following Sunday, she decided to take Hanna for another ride into the forest, or as she said to her mother, along the treeline. Entering the forest at the same point as last week, Saffron tried her best to take the same course, trying to provoke the same experience to happen.

But nothing did.

Birds chirped and tweeted, flapping and flying

about high up in the branches above. Sunlight streamed through the trees, bathing the green forest floor in golden streaks. At one point, she even saw a family of deer skipping through the trees in delight. The scenery around her was one of such tranquil beauty, Saffron found herself questioning whether she'd imagined the incident last week.

Frowning, but also quietly relieved, Saffron enjoyed a morning's ride with Hanna in nothing but peace. Later that evening, as she settled down in bed, Saffron picked up the story of James and Poppy once more.

Her mind wandered into enthusiastic fantasies of dark powerful creatures that loved their mates with such ferocious intensity. She thought of her mother and father, and how aside from the briefest of pecks on the cheeks, she'd never seen any exchange of affection between them. They moved around one another like old friends. Was that something just as comforting as the desperate need to kiss someone?

Saffron sighed. She'd never been kissed, never even had a crush on a boy, but a handful of boys had shown an avid interest in her. However, their childish displays of bravado, pushing each other around, climbing the biggest trees, lifting the heaviest things, did not impress Saffron at all. In fact, if anything, she cringed for them.

James though, despite only being seventeen,

seemed wise beyond his years. Saffron wondered if any boys like him existed for real or if what she sought would only ever be met in books. Combing through the pages with greedy hunger, as if it wasn't the third time she was reading it, Saffron soon found herself being lulled into a deep sleep, the book slowly tipping from her hand and falling onto the wooden floor...

*Saffron wandered through the forest. Blistering sunshine heated her pale skin. Around her, the trees thrived with life, bright green leaves in full bloom on their heavy branches. Baby birds hopped around the forest floor, trying in their earnest to learn to fly. To her right, a deer hopped and skipped through the undergrowth, its white tail bobbing up and down with its lively movements.*

*Sucking in a deep breath of fresh air, Saffron revelled in filling her lungs with the purity of nature. Whilst the City was fascinating, it could never replace the raw splendour of being somewhere like this.*

*Step by step, Saffron ambled through the picturesque forest, drinking in the glory of Mother Nature. A blur of movement caught her attention up ahead, followed by a striking colour that seemed unnatural amongst all the greens and browns of the environment around her.*

*Before she knew it, Saffron found herself running,*

*her legs stretching out in front of her in long ground swallowing strides. Her arms pumped at her sides as she hurried towards the bright red object rushing through the woods metres ahead of her.*

*As she darted through the trees, homing in on her target, it stopped moving. Saffron came to a standstill, bumping into a tree trunk to aid her sudden halt. Using the tree as a barrier, she peered around its wide girth to see what she'd been chasing. It was a boy. His white and red checked shirt had been what caught her attention.*

*Dressed in faded denim jeans and tan rigger boots, the boy turned around and looked straight at Saffron.*

*She gasped.*

*He wasn't a boy. He was a man. She narrowed her eyes, scrutinising every part of him—short cropped ash blond hair, wide set jaw, plump pink lips, broad muscled shoulders, and thick thighs, he was the very epitome of masculinity.*

*"Saffron," he said, his voice deep yet silky smooth.*

*A shiver ran through her.*

*The loud crunch of a twig snapping behind her had her whirling around in an instant. There stood the librarian, his smooth dark skin glistening under the sun's rays. He smiled at Saffron, a warm, welcoming smile that offered her nothing but reassurance.*

*Just as he opened his mouth to say something, a huge orange shape leapt from nowhere, smothering him in an instant. The librarian fell to the floor, his face hitting the ground with such force, it vibrated through Saffron's body.*

*Saffron stepped back, her hands flying to her mouth in fear. It was then her eyes focused on the thing that had attacked him. Black stripes, huge teeth, lethal head sized paws...it was a monstrous sized tiger.*

*It released its grip of the librarian's neck and looked up at Saffron. Amber eyes burned right through her, empty of a soul, devoid of any empathy or emotion. It licked its lips and opened its mouth, letting out a low, grumbling growl. Stepping over the mauled librarian, it padded towards Saffron, a prime example of lethal beauty.*

*Saffron backed up one step with each step the tiger took towards her. When her back met the rough bark of a tree, Saffron whimpered. The tiger roared, its predatory stare heightening Saffron's fear a hundred levels in less than a second.*

*It lowered down slightly then leapt through the air, its huge paws outstretched, reaching for her. Saffron screamed and closed her eyes...*

Saffron woke herself up screaming. She sat upright, covered in sweat and breathing like she'd just run a marathon. She patted herself down, making sure she was in fact still in one piece. The dream had been so vivid and lifelike, she was still processing the fact it wasn't her reality.

"It was just a dream," she whispered to herself. "Just a stupid dream."

She flopped back down onto her pillow, closing her eyes in sweet relief. When her heart rate slowed enough for her to consider sleeping once more, Saffron found herself thinking about the man in the red checked shirt. She realised, the more she thought about him, that he looked exactly like she pictured James to be, from her book.

"It's all Mia's fault," she said to herself, grinning. "Got me dreaming about fictional characters now."

Deciding it was time to stop reading before bedtime, Saffron closed her eyes and managed to enjoy a dream-free sleep.

CHAPTER EIGHT

As time passed by, Saffron eased into her teenage years, struggling through puberty and periods somewhat on her own. The nightmares she had remained with her, coming and going at random, but always the same. If it wasn't the darkness surrounding her in the forest, then it was the tiger killing Sam, the librarian.

Even though she had stopped reading before bedtime, Saffron knew, deep down in her gut, that these dreams were more than an overactive imagination. Not one detail ever faltered from these nightmares. It was almost as if they were a premonition.

As she became more self-sufficient and less reliant on her parents, she had the misfortune of being an overlooked child as her younger siblings demanded more time and attention from her mother and father.

Having grown into a quiet and thoughtful young lady, Saffron enjoyed her own company, spending her spare time reading. Her love for supernatural fiction had quickly evolved into a thirst for knowledge of myths and legends. Now the tender age of seventeen, Saffron had one more year of school before she was considered an adult member of Sehrstadt's community.

Following in her mother's footsteps, Saffron had spent the last four years learning the trade of being a seamstress.

"After all, sweetheart, who's going to do it once I'm gone?" Anna said to her.

Taming her wants to be an animal trainer, Saffron placated herself by teaching Henry tricks whenever she had spare time. She realised that if she wanted to make the town see that women could do the same jobs as men then she would have to wait until she was at least an adult.

The supply trips had become a regular monthly outing for Saffron. A friendship with Sam had soon bloomed as he grew accustomed to the Saturday's when Saffron would visit—always the first Saturday of the month. He would pick out new books he thought Saffron would enjoy and had never once failed in his selection.

Saffron's excitement of the City had quickly faded away. Aside from the extensive library, nothing of it appealed to her. The polluted air choked her, and the pompous clothes worn by the City folk made them resemble turkeys trussed up for Christmas dinner. No one seemed to have a moment for anyone; everyone was controlled by time, rushing from work to the shops, then back to work, shunning whatever may steal precious seconds of life.

To Saffron, this was no life. Life to her revolved around learning, soaking in the true beauty of the world around her, and helping nature bloom. She had quickly learned that the City had its perks—the schooling equipment, medical supplies, and fabrics made their life in Sehrstadt much easier. However, these small pros were not enough to lure Saffron from the safety and comfort of her cosy town.

When she read, Saffron had become an expert at blending into the background behind a stack of books. Usually, she would read down by Henry's field, giving her the view of staring straight up into the town. When her eyes became tired or strained, she would rest them by quietly watching the environment around her. Over time, she developed the guilty pleasure of people-watching.

It didn't take long for her to become amused at the people she'd grown to love and cherish. Just like the zombies in the City, people here, in Sehrstadt, were too caught up in their day-to-day tasks to notice what was happening right in front of them, to see a bigger picture unfolding.

A perfect example was Herr Humphrey Mayer, the resident lawyer who dealt with all manner of things from wills to land sales. His secretary was Hanna Hood, a beautiful young blonde just a year older than Saffron. With Humphrey being old enough to be her father, the idea of being attracted to the young woman repulsed him. But that didn't stop whispers from flying around the village, wondering what a lonely old man does all day shut inside a small building with a tempting young lady.

Saffron smirked whenever she heard this. They were correct, but only in the manner that he was lusting after someone and indulged in satisfying that desire three days a week. Everyone became so preoccupied and set on the idea that it was Hanna, no one batted an eyelid at his regular trips to Frau Becker, the village cook and baker.

The plump older lady was a jolly ray of life. Always smiling, cheeks permanently flushed red from laughter and a little too much wine, Sabine was nothing more than a widowed grandmother. Her infectious, deep giggles were enough to turn the saddest of souls into a smiling friend, and so in reality, it was no wonder the lonesome Humphrey turned to her for physical affection.

Similar to a magic show, people became so focused on one idea and proving themselves right, they often lost sight of what was actually happening in the background, where the *real* trickery lay. After all, why would Humphrey want a chubby, grey-haired grandmother when he could have a young, fertile virgin?

Saffron happened to still be a virgin. Not through lack of offers or opportunity but through choice. Despite their cut-off status from the world, some modern-day practices had leaked into their way of life, and that meant remaining pure until your wedding night was now a choice for the folk of Sehrstadt rather than a strict order.

As twilight gave way to the curtains of darkness that evening, Saffron didn't yet know just how that life choice might affect her.

CHAPTER NINE

Currently January, the last throes of winter were melting into the past, bringing a promising warm spring into the future. Weather in Sehrstadt was either beautiful and warm or bitterly cold. Seasons seemed to turn at the exact same time every year, as if it was pre-programmed into nature.

With it being the last day of the month and a Friday, tomorrow was the supply trip. The spring sun heated the icy breeze blowing across Sehrstadt today. Saffron's pink cheeks were wind-kissed, giving her a cute appearance as they contrasted against her otherwise pale skin.

Walking home from school, Saffron pulled her thick brown fur coat tighter around her, keeping the worst of the windchill off her. She found herself thinking about tomorrow and what wonderous books Sam would have picked out for her.

As she had grown older, Sam had seemed to instinctively know what direction Saffron's reading interest would go. By the time she was fifteen, whimsical ideals of fairytales were nothing more than hopeless dreams after he introduced her to the fables of the Brothers Grimm. The romantic promises of love, marriage, and children that Sehrstadt conditioned all young girls to was soon just a whisper of a false world to Saffron.

The dark twists, frightful monsters, and lack of happy endings brought the dawning realisation to her that the world she lived in contained these exact things. She quickly learned that if something seemed too good to be true, then it often was. A nagging feeling lay deep within her, quietly whispering that a dark secret lurked in the forest, one that was patient, ancient, and waiting for the next chance to strike.

It was impossible to ignore the fact that this year was the Offering. And Saffron had just celebrated her seventeenth birthday. From a quick calculation off the top of her head, another six girls would turn seventeen before the Offering which always happened on the autumn equinox—September 22$^{nd}$.

The man in the red checked shirt still visited her dreams. Since her birthday two weeks ago, he'd appeared to her every night. Always the same dream—where he reminded her of James from her books of younger years, and the librarian being mauled to death by a tiger.

Lots of wild animals lived in the woods, as the weekly hunting parties proved when they came back with spoils of pheasant, wild boar, and rabbit. However, there were definitely no tigers. Where this majestic, yet strange, character had interjected itself, she had no clue. What she did know was that the mind worked in mysterious ways and it either meant nothing at all or it meant as much as the appearance of the handsome man.

Saffron knew every line and crease on his face by now. For four years he had haunted her dreams, on and off. She had decided he wasn't a man, but neither a boy. It was as if he was stuck in some weird limbo with the body of a fully-grown man but the young fresh face of an older teenage boy, somewhere around her own age.

His green eyes had become a focal point for Saffron whenever she found herself in this dream. They were startling, almost glittering like gems, like they had a life of their own. Something about them hypnotised her more and more with each dream, as if he was trying to influence her in some way.

The next morning, after yet another visit from the

handsome man to her dreams, Saffron got herself ready for the usual supply trip. Mia still joined her, although her love for reading had waned as she'd gotten older. Promises of meeting previous Offering's had long since been forgotten about.

Whenever Saffron asked, she was met with the same response, "Not this time, Saffron. Maybe next time." As the months rolled by, she eventually gave up asking, but the fact she had been consistently steered away from this want had not slipped her mind.

The supply trips had been uneventful ever since that very first trip, four years ago. However, every time the wagon trotted deeper into the woods, Saffron couldn't shake the apprehension building inside her.

As always, when they reached the City, Saffron hopped off and headed straight for the library whilst the others went about collecting their own spoils along with the town's necessities. When she was eighteen, Saffron would be expected to gather items from whatever list she would be given. Then, she thought to herself, then she would meet the previous Offerings, but by then, the valuable insights they might be able to give her would be inconsequential.

Of course, Saffron had no idea if she would be chosen as an Offering or not. That wouldn't be decided until the actual day, but she firmly believed it couldn't hurt to be prepared. Knowledge is power, after all.

Walking quickly into the library, Saffron was greeted with a beaming smile from Sam. He was stood behind the desk on the ground floor, checking books in with his scanner. The high-pitched bleep sound it made always went through Saffron, making her shiver.

"Hi!" Sam said, putting his scanner down. "How are you?"

"Great, thank you. How are you?"

"All the better for seeing you, my dear. I have some fantastic books for you."

Saffron's eyes lit up like new-born stars. "What have you got?" she asked, placing her previous months books on the counter. Last month had been reading all about Norse mythology.

"A bit of a twist on mythology," Sam replied, leaning down underneath the counter. He stood up with six thick books all piled on top of each other. "Classic mythology. Much like your ancient such as Norse and Greek, but these are a bit closer to home."

Saffron rushed to the dark wooden counter, eagerly grabbing at the first book. "The History of Witchcraft and Demonology." She frowned and picked up the next, "The Werewolf in Lore and Legend." The creases in her forehead intensified as she read the title of the next one, "The Vampire: His Kith and Kin." She looked at the author name, noticing they were all from the same author, "Montague Summers." Glancing up at Sam, she gave him a puzzled look. "I went through the vampire phase when I first started coming here. Are you trying to make me re-visit my childhood?"

Sam laughed. "Not at all. What you read was fiction, my dear. These—" he placed a hand on top of the books "—are non-fiction."

"Non-fiction? As in true?"

Sam nodded. "Montague Summers was a Reverend. Not someone to be laughed at. He wrote over thirty books, most of them on witches, vampires, even demonology. He wholly believed in the supernatural and that it lives around us. His books are fascinating. Read them with an open mind."

"When exactly did this guy live?"

"Not that long ago," Sam said, a playful smile tugging at his lips. "He only died in 1948."

"Oh."

Sam laughed. "You were expecting hundreds of years ago, weren't you?"

Saffron grinned. "You can't blame me for thinking it."

"Just trust me. Shake off all your modern ideals and just embrace his literature. I promise, you'll enjoy it."

Keeping her doubts to herself, she said, "You know me, Sam. Always keen for the next book."

"I'll cut you a deal—if you don't like them, I'll quit my job."

Saffron's mouth fell open. "That's a bit dramatic, don't you think?"

"I pride myself in knowing people's reading tastes. If I can't do that anymore, then I may as well not be here, right?"

"Wow, ok. I'm not overly confident with you risking your life on me liking some books."

"You don't have to be confident. I do."

Saffron laughed. "Ok. I guess we'll see in a months time then."

"Have you got much time to sit and read today?"

Pulling her gold pocket watch out, a present that all sixteen year olds received from the town, Saffron checked the time. "Yes. I've got about thirty minutes."

"I cleared you a space over there," Sam said, pointing to a small table nestled at the back of the ground floor.

"Thanks, Sam."

Saffron made her way over to the sturdy mahogany coloured table. Two matching seats surrounded it, making it obvious that she would have this tiny space all to herself, unless some real inconsiderate human decided to come along and ruin it.

Plonking her stack of books down at one end, and sitting down at the other, Saffron made herself comfortable before getting stuck into *The Werewolf in Lore and Legend*.

"Excellent first choice," Sam said, giving her a cheeky wink as he replaced some books on the bookcases surrounding her.

Saffron smiled at him before getting stuck into the introduction. It was an annoying yet common theme with non-fiction books. However, this one had her grabbed by the fourth line. The author spoke of his original intentions to include information about various other were-animals including tigers, jaguars, lions, and leopards. He even mentioned hyenas and foxes.

Somewhat shocked, and definitely stunned, Saffron sat back and looked up at Sam. He was stood at the other end of the table, watching and grinning at her wildly.

"Does it look like I'm keeping my job?"

Saffron smirked. "All of these creatures? Really?"

Sam nodded. "I guess a better term for it would be shape-shifting, but technically that's wrong. A shape-shifter can move into any form, whereas those listed there are strictly limited to just that particular animal."

"A fox? A lion, a leopard..." Saffron's mouth was wide open in disbelief. "It never even entered my head that that could happen outside of a wolf."

"A lot of people don't think about it. The natural assumption has always been for wolves. I think because most native tribes are associated with them, but literally any creature you can think of, there will be a were-form of it."

"Even a crab?"

Sam burst out into laughter. "I've never found any literature about them, but anything is possible in this world, right?"

Dazed and her interest piqued, Saffron buried her head back in her book, eager to know more about this intriguing subject.

---

The author had a unique sense of writing. It was old school; lots of long sentences, intercepted with a questionable amount of commas, that made you forget the beginning of the sentence before you'd reached the end of it. It was mentally tiring reading it but so definitely worth it.

Saffron was quite glad when her half an hour was up and it was time to head back to the wagon. She needed a brief reprieve from the heavy concentration, and she hadn't even reached the end of the first chapter yet.

Pleased to see she wasn't the last one to reach the wagon, for a change, she climbed up into the back, taking an unusual seat near the front of the wagon. Frau Mueller and Frau Fischer were both seated opposite her, fussing over the white cloth that covered their supplies for the journey home.

Within a few minutes, everyone was back on board and heading back to their peaceful town. As they trotted down the winding country lanes, nearly back to the forest edge, some workmen had setup a tree cutting exercise on the side of the road. Splitting the already narrow road in half, they had placed some bright orange cones around their work area to keep passers-by out of harms way.

Their chainsaws roared and growled through the air as they sheared off overhanging branches from the road edge. As Herr Bauer guided the horses around the cones, a branch came tumbling down, crashing onto the road. Its long length caused it to spill out of the safe area of the cones, right into the path of their wagon. The horses merely stepped over it, it was barely half a foot thick, but the wheels on the old cart clattered and banged against it, causing everyone and everything to jolt around and come unstuck.

That included the supplies from under the white sheet at the front of the wagon.

Several parcels, wrapped in white greaseproof paper, came rolling out from underneath the sheet, hitting Saffron's left ankle and foot. She glanced down, frowning, and picked one of the smaller ones up.

Turning it over in her hands, she saw smears of blood on one side of the paper.

Frau Mueller and Frau Fischer were too busy repacking the fallen over fabrics and bags of flour to notice what Saffron had in her hand. As curious as ever, Saffron carefully undid the tape and opened the package.

When she saw a mound of freshly diced meat, she gasped.

Frau Fischer turned to her left, noticing the two remaining packages by Saffron's feet. Quickly re-taping the meat up, Saffron handed Frau Fischer the third package with a thin smile.

"Thanks, Saffron," she said, taking it from her like it was a fragile ornament.

Saffron didn't respond. Her mind was whirling, spinning at a hundred miles an hour. Why had they come to the City for meat? They had hunting parties go out every week into the forest. Why would we waste valuable resources for something the forest can provide for free?

Reasoning with herself that perhaps it was a just a treat, a one off that maybe one of the women wanted for their family, Saffron shooed any doubts and suspicions from her mind.

CHAPTER TEN

When they returned to Sehrstadt, Saffron decided, instead of immersing herself in her new books, she needed to relax and empty her mind. The only way for her to do that was to go riding.

Henry had now replaced Hanna in the daily routine up to the forge, meaning that Hanna had more or less been retired, save for the weekly ride that Saffron still took on a Sunday morning.

Carrying her saddle and bridle down to the paddock, Saffron whistled the old mare over. Hanna came cantering over, her ears pricked and nickering softly.

"I know I'm a day early, girl, but I really need it today."

Hanna rubbed her head up and down Saffron's

chest, signalling that she wanted a scratch under her forelock. Giggling, Saffron lifted up the flaxen wisp of hair and gave the old mare a tickle in her favourite spot. When she'd had enough, Hanna lifted her head and nudged at her saddle sat on the fence.

Saffron smiled as she tacked Hanna up, wondering if Henry would develop any of his mother's habits. So far, his training from Herr Schäfer had proved him to be nothing but a robot. Saffron hopes and prayed that would wear off as he grew older.

Although she didn't need the gate to reach Hanna's stirrups anymore, Saffron still used it as a mounting block, not wanting to hurt the old mare's back. As she was getting older, her muscles were naturally weakening and she didn't need any unnecessary strains and stresses.

Stepping off into a springing walk, Saffron headed Hanna towards the forest. Her mind wandered back to that day, four years ago, when she'd stumbled across the single paw print of a creature that definitely did not belong in the forest. For weeks after, she had religiously taken Hanna into the woods, scouring the ground for any hint of a track, but her efforts always proved fruitless.

Her interest had slowly evaporated and she put it down to stress of the situation making her think it was something it wasn't. The desire to ride inside the treeline had also been curbed after Herr Fuchs caught her riding one day and reported her to her parents. For months afterwards, her mother would watch her from their house, keeping a beady eye on her rebellious, hormonal teenage daughter.

Habit had soon formed, along with built in boundaries, and Saffron had soon found herself not even thinking about going inside the treeline. Along with her weird, recurring dreams, Saffron had tried her hardest to ignore the suspicions building in her mind.

Today though, after the incident in the wagon, all of Saffron's past experiences were spinning around her mind like a fairground carousel, trying to fall into place to explain something of some sort.

On a spur of the moment decision, Saffron decided to go into the forest today. With the hunting party already out and about, she would have to go deeper than ever before to avoid being seen. She urged Hanna into a trot and ploughed through the undergrowth, heading further and further inside the vast expanse of the mysterious forest.

The deeper they ventured, the closer together the trees became. Sunlight streamed through the bare branches, the deathly appearance of everything around her causing a violent shudder to jolt down her spine. Saffron dared to look behind her, seeing no hint of the way they'd just come in, despite the nakedness of the woods around her.

Trying to ignore the unease climbing in her chest, Saffron turned back to the front, mentally mapping the easiest path for her and Hanna to take. Lots of random evergreen bushes and thick hedges were planted out here, giving them easy cover should she happen to catch sight of the hunting party.

Saffron settled Hanna into a leisurely walk, taking in the scenery around her. After a couple of minutes, she realised that the forest was utterly silent. Was that because the hunting party was near? Had all the animals gone into hiding in fear of their lives?

Hanna's huge hooves rustled through the dead leaves covering the forest floor. The sound soon became so deafening to Saffron that she wished she could blow them all out of the way to stop it.

That was when Hanna stopped dead.

Saffron's heart leapt into her throat. She immediately scanned the forest floor around her. There, right in front of Hanna's legs, was a paw print.

"Sorry, girl," she said, jumping down from the mare's broad back.

Hanna stood stock still as Saffron hurried to the huge imprint on the forest floor. She bent down and placed her hand tentatively inside it. Her small hand barely filled the main pad, let alone reaching the remaining four pads and the claw marks.

"Wow," she breathed.

Looking ahead, she saw another one a few feet ahead. Scurrying towards it, she counted six steps before she reached it. From its position, more to the left than the first one, she realised that this was one stride—right front leg to left front leg.

"How big is this thing?" she whispered, totally awestruck.

She stood up, looking at the trail ahead of her—nothing but mud, crisp brown leaves, and a clear trail of monstrous sized paw prints. Running back to Hanna, she grabbed the mare's reins and clicked to her to walk forwards. Hanna refused to move.

A deep frown creased Saffron's forehead. She stood arguing with the mare for several minutes before she heard voices. Panic erupted inside her. Rushing to Hanna's side, she mounted up and turned Hanna back, the mare moving freely away from the unexplained paw prints.

Up ahead, she spotted a thick evergreen bush between two thick trees. Urging Hanna towards it, she positioned herself behind it, then dismounted and peered through the dense green leaves.

Two men came into view, Herr Weber and Herr Fischer. Herr Fuchs followed close behind with three other men Saffron couldn't quite see. Their raised jacket collars and large woolly hats made it difficult to pick out facial features.

A shrill whistle cut through the chat. "Here," Herr Weber yelled, beckoning for the rest of the party to join him.

Dread clamped around Saffron's heart like a vice. The tracks. They would see her tracks as well as the paw prints.

"There's hoof prints here..." Herr Fischer said, frowning.

"I'm not bothered about no damn wild horse," Herr Fuchs said. "I want this damn wolf. I want its head on a stake. Now."

Saffron's blood turned ice cold. A wolf. She stifled a gasp, putting her hand over her mouth. Wolves always ran in packs. Was there more than one? Was Sehrstadt at risk?

"Sir, with all due respect, we've been hunting this thing for years. What makes today any different to any other day?"

"I don't know, Peter," Herr Fuchs replied. "What made the day the war ended any different from any other day?"

Walter Fischer fell silent.

Saffron's pulse pounded through her ears. A wave of nausea, excitement, and apprehension tumbled around inside her. If they caught her, she would be in serious trouble. Time seemed to tick by with a painful slowness. Saffron looked at Hanna, pleased to see the old mare nodding off, not bothered by anything going on around her.

*At least there's no present danger*, she thought to herself.

"Follow the tracks," Herr Fuchs shouted to his men. "And you three, cover them up as we go."

Saffron watched, wide eyed in astonishment, as the three men at the back filled in the paw prints, patting down the earth to a smooth flat surface with shovels, leaving no trace of what had ever been there before.

Waiting for several minutes after they'd disappeared, Saffron eventually came out from under her cover. She tiptoed her way over to where the paw prints had been. Not one single track remained.

"What the...?"

Saffron made the decision that enough was enough —for today. Mounting Hanna, she quickly made her way towards what she thought was the treeline, the way she'd come in.

However, after riding for ten minutes in a straight line, Saffron came across a familiar looking evergreen bush stuck between two thick trees, and an unusually flat surfaced muddy path several metres in front of it.

"What the...?"

Confused, but trying to quash her rising panic, Saffron turned Hanna sharply to the left, heading her in a straight line for several minutes that way. When she came back to the same evergreen bush again, Saffron started to let fear take over.

"How can this be happening?" she said, pointing Hanna in a different direction and pushing her forwards that way.

Low and behold, ten minutes later, she was back at the same point. Terror coursed through her veins. She spun Hanna around on the spot, looking for a way out, some way, anything that pointed towards being the exit.

But everything looked the same. Dead tree after dead tree, interspersed with the odd evergreen bush, and a forest floor of mud, patterned with Hanna's hooves, back and forth.

Aware that the hunting party was still out here somewhere, Saffron bit down on her tongue to stop herself from screaming out loud. Tears welled up in her eyes. She leaned forwards, resting her forearms on the front of the saddle. Closing her eyes, she allowed a few tears to fall.

Hanna snorted and stomped her feet as she threw her head up and down. Saffron glanced up, catching sight of something in the distance. Desperate, she dug her heels into Hanna's sides, pushing the mare into a fast canter.

They bounded on, Hanna's big hooves thundering through the silent forest. Saffron kept her eyes pinned on the movement behind the evergreen bush in the distance, focused on the rustling leaves. As they approached, the leaves stopped rustling. Saffron held her breath.

Suddenly, to the right, a flurry of red dashed across Saffron's peripheral vision. She pulled Hanna to the right, heading her towards the bright colour moving through the bland colours of the forest. Clicking to the mare to pick up the pace, the wind whipped at Saffron's eyes, blurring her vision with tears.

The red blob turned into a hazy mark but its vibrant colour was still clear in Saffron's vision. Keeping it in vision, Saffron kept the mare on track, determined to catch it. All of a sudden, her mind whirled with the peculiar feeling of déjà vu. Her dream came back to haunt her, only this time in reality.

"No," she whispered, sitting back in the saddle and slowing Hanna down. "I wasn't riding in my dream."

Wiping at the stream of tears leaking from her eyes, Saffron cleared her vision, momentarily losing sight of the red mark. When she scanned the landscape ahead of her, looking for it, she panicked as she realised it wasn't there. It had vanished. Nothing could be seen at all.

But what she did see was the lush green grass of Sehrstadt, twenty metres out. Crying out in relief, Saffron picked up the pace again, desperate to reach safety once more. The second they emerged from the forest, at a flat-out gallop, Saffron let out a long breath and burst into tears.

CHAPTER ELEVEN

Saffron had the misfortune to think that her bad day was over. When she returned to the paddock, her father was back with Henry. Quickly patting at her eyes, she tried her best to look cheerful and just fine, but Walter was no fool.

"What's wrong, Saffron?"

"Nothing, Papa. Why?"

"Girl, don't treat me like a fool. Put the mare away and join me inside. We need to talk."

A lump of trepidation formed in Saffron's throat. Had her father seen her emerge from the forest? What could she use as an excuse? Or should she just be honest?

She wanted to take her time tending to Hanna, to delay the inevitable, but at the same time, she knew her father wasn't a patient man. Promising Hanna she would come back in a bit with her feed, she hurried indoors to find her father sat in his beloved chair, reading a newspaper. The open fire crackled next to him, the orange flames fiercely licking at the pile of logs he'd thrown on.

From his wooden, hand-carved chair—lined with boar skin for comfort—Walter tore his attention from the newspaper, folded it up neatly, and placed it on the chair arm. He enjoyed keeping a track of modern events occurring in BlauPferd. The fact the papers were out of date by the time he got them didn't bother him. It gave him something to do when he needed time away from work and his family.

Leaning forwards, he looked up at Saffron and said, "Your mother is out. Now, tell me what's going on, dear girl? I am not as blind as you may think."

"I...what do you mean?"

His grey eyes darted towards the doorway before settling back on his daughter. "I know you've been in the forest, Saffron. More than once."

Saffron's mouth ran dry. Her throat closed up. A hurricane of words and excuses spun around her mind, but nothing settled enough for her to form a coherent sentence.

"You know, don't you?" Walter said.

Saffron's heart thumped against her ribcage. A

burst of adrenaline shot through her bloodstream, spiking her senses. "I...I...know what?"

A light-hearted chuckle sounded from the old man. Nearing sixty, he had been late in life starting a family, but he had only wanted to do so under the right circumstances and with the right woman. He'd explained this to all his children in an effort to make them appreciate the sanctity of relationships.

Saffron knew that her mother was twelve years younger than her father. Anna had explained that she wanted to explore life and what it had to offer her before settling down with a husband to start a family. She had been thirty before falling pregnant with Saffron, but as she was wholly satisfied with her life up to this point, she lived for her children rather than wishing she had opportunities to do things the children now prevented her from doing.

"Dear girl," Walter said, beckoning his daughter towards him. "You have more of me inside that head and heart of yours than you'll ever know. Come on now, don't take me for a fool."

Her breath caught in her throat as she debated playing the dumb card. After a few seconds, she glanced down at the wooden floor and nodded. "I know something isn't right, Papa. I just don't know what."

Walter smiled. "I didn't think it would get past

you. You're too clever for your own good. What do you know?"

"I know we're not allowed to meet previous Offerings. I know I've seen wolf tracks in the woods. I know I've seen meat being brought back on the supply trip. I know that the hunting party isn't hunting wild boar and pheasants. The Offerings...are they even real? Because I'm beginning to think otherwise. What is going on?"

"I cannot say too much," he replied. "My realistic views are often not appreciated around here, and I don't just mean your mother."

Saffron frowned, alarm bells already ringing in her head. "What is it?" she whispered, her question almost a breathless gasp. "What happens to the girls who go into the forest?"

The wise old man pulled his lips into a thin line. "They are sacrificed."

The sharp gasp Saffron made almost choked her. Instant fear flooded her. "For...for what?"

"Not for what, dear girl. *To* what." He licked his lips and rubbed his hands over his face. When he made eye contact with his daughter again, his shadowed eyes were full of fear. "It is a creature so hideous I cannot even begin to describe it. The mere thought of it sends shivers down my spine." As if to prove a point, he shuddered. "It is big, Saffron. Its size would tower over both of our horses put together."

Thinking of the size of Henry and Hanna, Saffron wanted to call her father a liar. Nothing could be as big as that, not within these parts, surely? Someone would have seen it before now.

"But that's not all, Saffron. Its teeth are many, and their sharpness would rival any blade. It has claws like talons from an eagle, and its thirst for blood is greater than any animal I know."

All the colour drained from Saffron's face. Assuming her father was speaking from legends and myths, she couldn't help her response. "You're wrong... You have to be. It can't be true."

Walter smiled at his daughter. Glancing quickly towards the closed door, he turned in his chair and lifted the side of his shirt.

When Saffron saw the ugly, red scars across the left side of his body, she jerked backwards. Four scratch marks the length of a ladle disfigured his flesh from his shoulder blade diagonally down to the front of his left hipbone. The puckered scars still looked as red and angry as if they'd been done yesterday.

"Wh...what happened? Are you telling me you've met this thing?"

"That I have, dear girl. I attempted to kill it. My

sister happened to be one of its Offerings. She had a suspicious mind, just like me. When she was chosen, we hatched a plan where I would meet her on one of the hunting trails and go with her. We had everything accounted for—except *it*. We knew it would be some sort of beast, but I expected a bear at worst. I'd been out into the forest a few days before and dug out a pit, filling the bottom of it with wooden spikes. The idea being to lure the creature towards my sister and have it fall in the trap."

Saffron swallowed the dry lump in her throat. "Did it not go in the trap?"

"Oh, it went in the trap," Walter replied, smiling. "And it walked straight back out."

"What?" Saffron's mouth hung wide open.

"That pit was ten feet deep, eight feet long, and eight feet wide. We heard the wooden stakes pierce its body. It howled in pain. We saw blood spurt upwards. But seconds later, it jumped out like nothing had happened. I could see its wounds, Saffron. I saw straight through its body and right before my eyes, that hole sealed up like it had an invisible zip."

Tears sprung to Saffron's eyes. A bitter, metallic taste lingered on her tongue. Beads of sweat formed on her palms and around her face, cooling her with their icy presence. It took her a minute to realise her entire body was quivering. Nausea rolled around in her stomach like the clothes she washed in the dolly tub.

"But...but that's not possible," she whispered. "It can't be."

"I had other weapons with me, in case the pit trap failed. Nothing worked on it, dear girl. Not the shotgun I had, the machete, or the spear I lodged through its heart. It all seemed to just piss it off more."

"So how did you escape? What happened to your sister?"

Her father gave a sad smile. Water glistened over the wistful look in his eyes. "I like to think she made it to the City, but I'll never know for sure. The only reason I'm alive today is because something frightened that creature away. After it swiped me here"—he placed his hand on his left side—"it froze mid-air as it took aim for my throat. It spent a few seconds sniffing the air, gave me one last look, growled, and bolted."

"What scared it off?"

Walter shook his head. "I can't say for certain. The pain from this wound was like white hot agony. I've had some injuries in my time, dear girl, especially working in the forge, but I can tell you that this is the most painful thing I have lived through. The excruciating pain sent me delirious, I couldn't see straight." He paused and looked at the floor. "I can't be sure if the glimpse of what I saw was real or an illusion."

Saffron sat bolt upright. "What? What was it, Papa?"

Lost in old memories, Walter stared straight ahead, as if back there all that time ago, experiencing the same thing all over again. "I thought I saw a cat."

"Like Mouser?" Saffron asked, thinking of their tabby female who kept the barn and feed shed pest free.

"No, no, no. A *big* cat. Flashes of orange and black and an almighty roar are what stick in my mind, but after that, I passed out. The next time I woke up, I was in someone's log cabin out in the woods."

"Whose?"

"I don't know. I tried so many times to find my way back there but never succeeded. I just ended up going around in large circles. But I remember waking up inside this small hut, laid on my back on a table. An old lady dabbed at my wounds, telling me I would be okay. She was drawing the venom out of my blood. I know it was real. I still remember the crackling of damp logs on the open fire, the sting of my flesh as she placed gauze over my wounds, and I can still smell the delicious stew she had on the stove. I know it happened. The last meal she fed me was the most delicious venison pie. I haven't eaten that since I was a boy. Your mother hates it. I *know* it was real."

He banged a clenched fist on his knee, his

knuckles white and his teeth scraping together. Saffron took a minute to soak in his words. A cat? Orange and black? That would be a tiger...but they don't roam these parts. An old woman in the forest in a log cabin? Someone would have come across her dwelling by now, surely?

"What happened next?" she asked, curious what the rest of the village would say about his curious tale.

"I found myself atop Hanna's mother, Adele, good old mare she was. I came to just as we rode into the market square. When I collapsed on the ground, a story of a bear attack rolled off my tongue—the wounds proved it. What I couldn't prove was the old lady who'd saved me. The doctor eventually asserted that I'd dreamed of comfort and being tended to as my body fought the infection. When I was strong enough, I'd found my way back to Adele and ridden back to the village. Apparently, I hadn't been seen for almost a week. They'd sent search parties looking for me but found no trace of me, let alone anything that happened."

"That is kind of plausible."

"Perhaps," he said, shrugging his shoulders. "Except I never took Adele with me in the first place. In fact, my uncle had been ploughing his vegetable patch with her just that morning when I reappeared. He'd left her hitched up to the plough whilst he went to fetch a pail of water. When he came back, she had simply vanished."

Saffron's jaw dropped. Something extremely peculiar was happening here. Were her father's stories true or were they just the ramblings of a wounded man caught in the illusion of a heated infection?

CHAPTER TWELVE

That night, Saffron was afraid of going to sleep. She knew, after her father's story, that what would come to her in her dreams would be a mangled frightening mess of what he'd shared with her...

*Standing in the middle of the forest, Saffron looked around her. Above her, the moon shone in all its glory, full and round, casting a bright silver glow over the earth. She noticed the trees in full bloom, the canopy of leaves and branches thick overhead, yet somehow, the lunar light penetrated the dense foliage.*

"*Saffron.*"

*The silky-smooth voice had her whirling around in a second, but there was nothing to see.*

"*Saffron.*"

*She spun around again, still seeing nothing.*

*"Saffron."*

*Turning around and around, Saffron soon made herself dizzy. She shouted in frustration, "What do you want? Who are you?"*

*Despite now standing still, Saffron's world still moved around her, the effects of the dizziness grasping a firm hold of her. When everything stopped moving, she slowly glanced to her left. She screamed. A pair of big brown eyes stared at her, a thick band of grey fur separating them.*

*Saffron stumbled backwards. As she did so, the intense moonlight enabled her to see more of the face mere feet from her own. An elongated snout, giant pointed ears, a leathery black nose...*

*"Oh my goodness," she whispered, tears of fear springing up from nowhere.*

*The wolf opened its mouth, revealing a jaw full of enormous teeth and two gigantic canines. Saffron fell over, scrabbling away from the looming head of the massive wolf. It took one step, placing both paws either side of Saffron's head. A sliver of drool slid off one of its canines, landing on the ground next to her head.*

*It lowered its head, its hot breath blowing over Saffron's face. Saffron raised her arms to protect her face, squeezing her eyes shut as she waited to be ripped to pieces...*

Gasping for breath, Saffron sat bolt upright, covered in sweat. She realised now that this beast was taunting her in her dreams, revelling in the fact it could kill her over and over. Stubborn determination ignited in her veins.

Slowly calming her heart rate, Saffron eased herself back onto her pillows. She realised that despite the other girls who would be in the running for this 'prestigious' position of being an Offering, her sixth sense told her this was going to be her turn.

Whether she liked it or not.

And so she lay there, wide awake, until dawn broke, thinking of ways to best this beast.

---

Saffron decided the first thing she needed to do was focus on her physical fitness and strength. That morning, she rose, just as the first rays of light broke through the last of the night and headed out for a jog. By the time she was halfway around the perimeter, she was doubled over, wheezing for breath. Fury and the will to not give in pushed her on, forcing her to finish her run.

Reminding herself that she would only find this easier with each day that passed, Saffron swore to herself that she must do this every morning, come rain or shine. Being so close to the treeline as well would allow her to pick out certain patterns or markers in the trees, making it easy for her to spot her way out, should she need to.

She knew once she went in the forest, she'd lose all sense of direction and navigation. Leaving a trail of breadcrumbs hadn't worked so well for Hansel and Gretel, so the idea hadn't even been in contention with her. Attaching ribbons to trees or shrubbery would only give away her lack of faith in her town and her people, and that wouldn't be well received.

When Saffron returned home, she took a long bath, soothing her aching muscles. Then, she headed into the kitchen and made herself a bowl of steaming porridge whilst putting some rolls in the oven for the rest of her family.

Much to her surprise, her father waltzed into the kitchen just as she scraped the last of her oats into her mouth.

"Good morning, Saffron," he said, placing the kettle on the stove. "You're up early today."

"I know I'm next, Papa," she said, bluntly.

Walter raised an eyebrow, silently asking his daughter a question.

"The Offering. I know I'm next."

"How do you possibly know that?"

Saffron sighed, then confessed her darkest secret. "I've been having dreams, dreams of a beast in the forest. Last night they intensified by a hundred. I know it's me. It's taunting me, showing me what's going to happen when I get out there."

"How do you know this isn't affecting the other girls who are seventeen this year? How do you know it's not visiting their dreams?"

Saffron shrugged her shoulders. "I don't. It's just a hunch. But I'm pretty convinced."

The kettle whistled, cutting through their conversation. Saffron drank her glass of milk, mulling things over in her mind. When her father took a seat opposite her with his cup of coffee, Saffron dared to ask a dangerous question.

"Papa, would it be possible to perhaps learn some of your smithery?"

"Now why would you want to learn that?" he asked, narrowing his eyes in suspicion. "The forge is no place for a woman, lesser so for a young girl."

Saffron shrugged her shoulders. "I'm curious about how you make things. It's intrigued me for a long time."

"Daughter, we had a heart to heart yesterday. Please do not go back to thinking I am unwise to your plans."

Saffron frowned. "What plans?"

"There is a reason you want to learn smithery only

now. What is it?"

Swallowing the lump in her throat, Saffron closed her eyes and whispered, "I want to craft a blade, one lethal enough to take out the beast."

Walter leaned back in his chair and laughed. "I admire your spirit, dear girl, I really do. But no blade could take out that thing. Did you not listen to my story?"

"Yes, Papa. But I cannot go in unarmed. I need to have something, even if it won't kill it, but at least to maim it. Anything that can help me in any way."

"Saffron, you probably won't survive the first night. You do know this?"

A bolt of terror shot straight through her. Suspecting something and having it confirmed were two entirely different things. "That doesn't mean I can't go down without a fight, right?"

Walter pursed his lips.

"Consider it a dying girl's last wish?"

Her father sighed. "Ok. It's Sunday today, my day off. Come to me tomorrow, after school. I'll start teaching you the basics."

Saffron wanted to throw her arms around her father and thank him, but she knew that would do nothing but make him uncomfortable. Instead she just said, "Thank you, Papa," and kept her screams of joy internal.

CHAPTER THIRTEEN

Saffron was elated at her father agreeing to show her how to forge her own blade. School slid by in a slow, torturous hell, almost as if time itself was mocking her. Eventually, the final bell rang and Saffron was free.

Running all the way across town and beyond, Saffron decided it was an extra spurt of fitness that would do her no harm. Some of the townsfolk gave her curious glances as she sped past them, wondering what had her in such a desperate rush.

*They'll understand soon enough* she thought to herself.

By the time she reached the forge, Saffron had just started to feel the now familiar burn in her lungs when her body was at its limit. She smiled to herself and decided it felt good, it reminded her she was alive.

"I'm here, Papa," she said, bursting through the small personnel door on the side of the huge wooden workshop.

The instant she entered, a wall of heat hit her, rocking her back on her heels. "Wow," she breathed. Suddenly catching her breath in such humid conditions became a difficult task.

Walter walked over to her, chuckling. "Bit warm for you?"

"That's insane. How do you work in this heat?"

"You get used to it. It's lovely in the winter, not so much in the summer."

Saffron raised her eyebrows. She hadn't even thought about working in this during sweltering heat waves.

"Did you bring a change of clothes?" Walter asked.

Saffron nodded.

"You can get changed over there."

Saffron followed his pointed finger to a huge water butt. It must have been the size of a car. Seeing that made Saffron notice just how big of a place her father's forge was. It was essentially an old barn, the ceiling metres above her, coming together in a traditional pointed shape. Easily ten metres wide and fifteen metres long, they could fit their entire house in here and have room left over.

In the centre stood a huge brick-built pit with heaps of coal glowing red hot in the middle and thick orange flames dancing about on top.

"Is that it?" she asked, pointing to it. "Is that where I'm going to make my blade?"

Walter nodded. "That's the forge. But we've got lots to learn before then."

Not needing to be told twice, Saffron hurried over to the water butt, changing into her old clothes as fast as she possibly could. She emerged, grinning wildly.

"Basics today, Saffron," her father said. "We're not forging anything for a little while yet."

Her heart dropped to her feet but she understood she needed to learn about processes, tools and vital rules before even picking up a block of metal.

Over the next two weeks, Saffron learned everything about working in a forge, from tongs and rasps to bellows and swage blocks. She watched her father create all manner of things from horseshoes to swords to hammers, her eyes always wide open in fascination.

The ghastly wolf still haunted her dreams, every night, without fail. Dread of sleeping had taken a hold of her to begin with, but now she was almost welcoming of its frightful, monstrous head, looming over her. She refused to let it intimidate her and turned her throat-closing terror into drive and determination to beat this thing, one way or another, whatever the cost.

Her physical fitness was improving everyday which she noticed herself when she ran to the forge after school, puffing less and less with each time. Today, Saffron was watching her father create something in the forge. She frowned as she tried to see what exactly he was making.

Two circular shaped ends were joined by a slender middle, just about long enough for a hand to grip the middle of.

"Papa, what are you making?"

Walter grinned as he hammered the strange object into the shape he desired. After nearly an hour of beating the hot metal, he dropped it in the cooling tank and then presented it to Saffron.

"Don't think I haven't noticed your morning runs, Saffron," he said. "You need more than just being able to run to stand any chance of fighting this thing."

Saffron frowned. "What do you suggest?"

"You need strength. This beast is fast, Saffron. It may be big, but it moves with the speed and reflexes of a deer. This—" he said, pointing to the strange shaped object "—is called a weight. City folk use them in their gymnasiums."

Memories of learning about the City's culture

years ago at school sprung forward, flooding Saffron's mind. "Of course. I remember now. Dumb bells aren't they also called?"

Walter smiled. "Yes, well done. I'm making you your own set so you can build up your muscles. It's no use being able to run if you can't climb a tree."

Realisation dawned in Saffron's mind. Her father was right. "Thanks, Papa. I really appreciate this."

"When they become to easy to lift, I'll make you a heavier set."

Saffron couldn't hide the grin spreading over her face. Her father spent the next hour showing her different exercises and ways to warm up and cool down, properly.

"How do you know all this?" she asked him. "We never learned the ins and outs of City folk's training regimes at school, just the basics of what they do in their gymnasiums."

Walter gave his daughter a crooked smile. "With age comes wisdom and experience, dear girl. You'll collect your own treasure chest of knowledge as you progress through life."

Frowning at his cryptic answer but thinking no more of it, Saffron revelled in all the information her father was freely giving to her. As she settled herself down to sleep that night, she couldn't help but think how her impending death sentence had somehow developed the relationship with her father to a whole new level she never thought possible.

For the first time in a long time, Saffron fell asleep with a warm smile on her face.

CHAPTER FOURTEEN

When the next supply trip came around, Saffron very nearly missed it. Just as the wagon pulled out of the town square, she ran after it, yelling and waving at Frau Mueller for her to stop it.

"You're late, Saffron," she said, offering her a hand up into the back.

"I'm sorry. I've been in the forge with Papa."

"Yes, I've noticed you spending a lot of time in there lately. Is everything alright?"

Saffron offered the woman a small smile. "Perfectly fine."

Thankfully, Frau Mueller didn't push the conversation any further. Saffron had wanted to stay in the forge with her father. She'd actually been crafting her very first piece of metalwork—a horseshoe, but it was something at least. However, she felt she owed Sam an explanation as to why she hadn't read his books yet, rather than just not turning up and making him worry he'd incorrectly trusted in her.

Nerves churned around inside her as she thought about his reaction to her not bringing the books back. Would he be angry? Would it get him in trouble? Saffron chewed her lip the whole ride there, anxiety taking control of her. The journey there seemed to take forever and by the time the wagon finally stopped, Saffron was a jittery mess.

She walked into the library, sheepish, and her mind spinning with ways to word her poor excuse.

"Hi," Sam said, giving her a beaming grin. "How are you?"

"I'm good, thank you. How are you?"

"All the better for seeing you," he said, looking at her empty arms. He raised an eyebrow. "Did you forget something?"

Saffron's cheeks flared with heat. "I'm really sorry, I just haven't had time to read as much these past few weeks. I've been really busy preparing for a big event and my reading has just taken a backseat. I'm so sorry. Can I keep them another month? Please?"

"Of course you can. I'll just move the due date on the system so it doesn't flag up. Plus, the fact you didn't bring them with you kind of leaves me with no choice..." He flashed her a cheeky grin.

"I'm sorry," she said, pressing her hands to her cheeks in an effort to calm the burn of her skin. "I kind of had a feeling that you wouldn't mind..."

"You're right, I don't mind at all. So, this big event, what is it? Tell me more."

Saffron jerked her head back, completely taken aback by his interest in her town's goings on. She hesitated, not sure how much she could say. "It's just this stupid thing we do every once in a while to honour our forest gods."

Well aware that gods were a 'thing' in the City, Saffron figured phrasing it that way instead of as forest spirits would be better received.

"Nice," Sam replied, nodding his head. "So what do you do to honour them?"

Saffron cleared her throat and said, "We have a... there's a monument in the middle of the forest to them. We take gifts out to it."

"Cool. What sort of gifts?"

Folding her arms over her chest, Saffron suddenly felt rather defensive and really didn't want to answer too many questions on the subject. "Just food and things."

Sam pursed his lips and looked away, disappointment settling over his dark features. Saffron couldn't help the wave of guilt rising in her. He was a nice guy and she knew she'd just cut him down with this conversation. He was only showing an interest, after all.

"I...I err need to go. The wagon will be leaving soon."

"See you next month?"

Saffron nodded and fled from the library like a scolded cat. The wagon wouldn't be leaving for at least another half an hour. She suspected Sam knew that, but it severed the questions about the Offering, saving Saffron some awkward moments.

## CHAPTER FIFTEEN

By the time May came around, Saffron was nothing like her former self of only a few months ago. Strong, athletic, with lithe muscles, she was only face paint away from being some sort of female warrior. She devoured meat and vegetables like it was going out of fashion, she ran everywhere she possibly could, and she spent every spare moment with her father in the forge, making an array of weapons.

At this point, she had made half a dozen poaching traps, dozens of thick, sharp nails, and a length of chain that was enough to wrap a whale up in.

She'd noticed the people of her community giving her inquisitive looks, watching what she was doing, whispering to one another. Saffron tried her best to ignore them, placating herself with the justification that soon enough, they would understand.

Having still not read the pile of books that Sam had picked out for her back in January, Saffron had skipped out on the last few supply trips. Guilt gnawed at her insides. She knew that by now, Sam must have been reprimanded or punished in some way for lending an outsider precious books that had no guarantees of being returned.

The dreams had lessened somewhat over the last few weeks. Saffron convinced herself it was because she was becoming stronger, mentally and physically. She hoped the beast could sense it and had backed off trying to scare her.

This morning, however, Saffron decided she needed to join the supply trip and make amends with Sam. Collecting all of the books into her arms, she slid them inside the hessian sack she used for carrying her spoils and headed over to the waiting wagon.

Mia waved at her excitedly from the back of the cart. "Hey!"

Saffron jumped up into the back of the wagon with ease, not needing any help. "Hi, Mia."

"Wow, look at you. You're so...fit. What's been going on?"

Saffron shrugged her shoulders. "Not much. I'm just trying to be the best version of myself that I possibly can be."

Mia nodded, smiling in approval. "Makes sense.

I've noticed you running a lot lately and spending a lot of time with your father."

"He's teaching me how to make things in the forge."

Mia's eyebrows raised. "That's so cool! How did you convince him to do that? He's always so...strict about what men do and what women do."

"I just asked him and he said yes. It's been fascinating. I've loved it."

"What have you made?"

Saffron knew she couldn't tell her friend the truth. "Oh, just the usual. Horseshoes, tools, that kind of thing."

"Have you burned yourself yet?"

"No, not yet. Papa makes sure I'm really well protected. It's so hot in there though. In the winter it was absolute bliss, I never wanted to leave, but now the weather is warming up, it's practically unbearable."

Mia grinned. "And it's only May. It's going to get hotter yet."

The wagon lurched forwards, jolting both girls from their conversation. As they trotted through the forest, Mia leaned forwards and whispered, "Do you remember your first ever supply trip?"

Saffron's blood turned ice cold. Of course she did. "Sort of, why?"

"I can't ever pass through here without thinking about that day. It was so...odd."

Not knowing the best way to deal with this, Saffron decided to feign ignorance. "What was so odd?"

"Don't you remember? The horses freaked out and you jumped down to see what was going on. Then that wind came along...and said your name."

Saffron closed her eyes and shivered, as if she were reliving that terrifying moment all over again. "It was just a trick of the mind, that's all. Nothing else. We were all creeped out because of the horses acting strange."

Mia pulled her lips into a thin line and then sat back, her eyes studying Saffron carefully. Saffron felt bad. If she ever needed a friend to confide in, Mia would be a good ally, and now would be the time to gather some support.

"Come with me to the library," Saffron said, lifting her brow in such a way to indicate conspiracy.

Mia's disappointed look turned into a cheeky grin. "I would love to."

The rest of the trip to the City was nothing more than slow, lingering torture as the truth of Saffron's situation bubbled on the end of her tongue, desperate to burden someone else with the harsh reality.

The wagon had barely stopped before the two girls were leaping from the back, rushing to the library.

Apprehension filled Saffron with every step as she awaited the wrath of Sam to hit her full force.

Mia opened the front door, allowing Saffron to pass through first. Hesitant but knowing she had yet to face much worse fates, Saffron held her head high, squared her shoulders, and walked right in.

"Hey," said Sam.

Saffron looked to her left to see him stocking some shelves. "Hi," she said, her cheeks burning red. "I'm so sorry I've disappeared the last few months, I've just been so busy—"

Sam held a hand up. "It's ok, Saffron. You don't need to explain yourself to me. I know things from your neck of the woods aren't as straight forward as our way of life. Have you read them all yet?"

Hanging her head in shame, Saffron said, "No...I brought them back because I didn't want you to get into any more trouble."

Sam walked over to her and placed a hand on top of the books. "You keep hold of them until you're done with them. Don't you worry about me."

The door banged shut behind Saffron, making her jump. Sam turned to the noise, his face cracking into a beaming grin when he saw Mia.

"Mia," he breathed. "It's so good to see you again."

Saffron turned to look at her friend, noticing the pink blush flushing across her cheeks. She watched with acute interest as Mia and Sam spoke to one another, big warm smiles never leaving their faces.

After several minutes of catching up, Mia turned to Saffron and said, "Shall we?"

Saffron, bemused by her friend's obvious affections for the librarian, nodded and headed up the stairs, carrying her books with her. They sat at one of the tables they used to read their supernatural teenage books at.

"What's going on?" Mia whispered, lowering her head as she spoke. "Tell me everything."

Taking a deep breath, Saffron spent the next fifteen minutes filling Mia in on all the details of what had been going on in her life. It was only as she shared all the details of her nightmares, her experiences in the forest, and everything else, that Saffron began to realise she was in much deeper than she originally thought.

"We're going to have to set traps," Mia said, her voice still hushed. "We can go into the forest at night and leave markings on trees, discreet ones that only we know about, so you know where the traps are. We can lay string for you to find your way out too. There are ways around it, Saffron."

Not the reaction she was expecting from Mia, Saffron couldn't help but stare at her friend with her mouth wide open. "Are you not surprised at all about all of this? That the hunting party doesn't bring our meat? That there's a beast stalking the woods?"

Mia shrugged her shoulders. "It doesn't take much to realise that the way we live and the way most of society lives is very different. There are reasons for it. Plus..." she looked around her, making sure they were alone "...I kind of found something, a few years ago, in the town hall archives."

"What?" Saffron replied, moving her head in closer to Mia. "What did you find?"

"I started working with Herr Schulz, to make more room in the basement. He asked me to box up all of their old records ready for them to go into storage in the attic. It got really boring and tedious so to break up the monotony of it, I started looking through some of the stuff. I found a bunch of pictures of previous Offering's. I got curious and looked through the files—they all had death certificates stamped the day of the Offering—of the next one, seventeen years after they went into the forest."

Saffron gasped. "No."

Mia nodded. "I bet if we found the file of the last girl who went into the forest, there wouldn't be a death certificate...not for another four months anyway."

"Are you suggesting that we break into the town hall?"

Mia grinned.

"But if that is the case, then that means that whatever is going on, the adults know about it."

"Not necessarily all of them, but the most prominent, definitely."

Saffron nodded. "I think you're right. There's something going on here and I'm determined to find out what. Are you with me?"

Flashing her friend a beaming smile, Mia said, "Did you even need to ask?"

CHAPTER SIXTEEN

It was midnight when Saffron slipped out of her bedroom and snuck across the silent, empty grassland of her town. The moon hung high in the sky, covering the earth in silvery light. She moved swiftly, brushing along the buildings for cover, just in case any residents happened to be up and about with eagle eyes.

Breaking out into the wide-open space of the town square, she hurried towards the far end, where the town hall sat. Mia was crouched down by the side of the building, waiting for her friend.

"Here," she whispered, motioning for Saffron to hurry. "Through the back entrance."

The two girls rushed to the back of the large wooden building, quietly opening the small wooden door that led straight into the basement.

"I never knew this was here," Saffron said, noticing how the door blended into the wall perfectly.

"It's supposed to be a fire exit, in case anyone is trapped in the basement and a fire starts overhead. They made it look like part of the wall so nobody could do what we're doing."

Saffron giggled. When Mia opened the door, revealing the depth of the blackness that awaited them, Saffron couldn't help but step back.

"Are you crazy? We'll fall down the stairs!"

Mia opened her thin jacket to reveal a torch. She grinned and pressed the button, illuminating the rickety set of stairs ahead of them.

"Where did you get that?" Saffron breathed.

"I found it in my dad's tools. Seems modern day lighting is allowed for some."

As Mia took the lead down the wooden staircase, a soft breeze blew over Saffron, covering her in goosebumps. She shivered and dared to look behind her at the treeline. Nothing obvious stared back at her but the overwhelming sense that something was watching her made her not want to turn her back and descend down the stairs.

"Shut the door behind you," Mia whispered. "We can get back out easily."

Saffron stepped inside the door and closed it,

facing outwards, just in case something broke free from the trees and ran for her.

"Come on," Mia said, her voice echoing up from the bottom.

Hurrying down the poorly lit staircase, Saffron tried to push her irrational fears from her mind. If she was feeling like this, in familiar territory, and with a friend, how on earth was she going to cope in the forest on her own?

Mia grabbed her hand and frogmarched her to the back of the musty smelling basement. Saffron gazed around her, surprised at how the set up down here was very much like a library. Dozens of handmade bookcases stood feet apart, reaching up to the low ceiling that Saffron could easily touch if she lifted her hand above her hand.

"Personnel records are over there," Mia said, pointing to the far-right corner. "Town history, buildings, and all that nonsense are in the middle here, and over there..." she pointed to the far left "...is all the 'miscellaneous' as Herr Schulz called it. That's where I found all the stuff on the previous Offerings."

Saffron almost needed to run to keep up with Mia's long, hurried strides. The cold concrete floor beneath her feet did not escape her attention. She began to realise that much more of modern life lay in the very foundations of her beloved town than what the adults wanted the children to know about.

Heading into the far corner, Mia kneeled down and began picking through cardboard boxes. "I can't remember the name of the box I found all the files in," she said. "It was something really obscure. Something you wouldn't have ever thought would contain what it did. We'll have to pick through them all, one by one. You're looking for creamy coloured folders with names on the front of them. You'll know them when you see them, trust me."

Saffron bent down and lifted the lid off the dirty white box closest to her. She flicked through piles of black and white photographs, not taking much notice of them. That was until she came across one that was slightly larger than the rest. The face in the middle of the photo smiled back at her until she lost all the breath in her body.

"Oh my goodness," she said, almost choking. "This...this is my *papa*. Mia, Mia, look at this!"

Mia scurried over to her friend and took the photo from Saffron's shaking fingers. Turning it over she flashed the torchlight over the date written in curly handwriting on the back—1949.

"That would make your papa seventy," she said, frowning. "I don't understand. He looks exactly the same here as what he does every day."

Saffron's gut churned over with a bad feeling. Dread, anxiety, and oppression all mixed together inside her. "How is this possible?"

"Maybe it's his father. You know how some fathers and sons can look similar."

"That isn't similar," Saffron said, stabbing her finger at the figure in the photo. "That is my papa."

Mia shook her head. "No," she said. "There will be a rational explanation for it, I'm sure." She threw the photo back in the box. "That's not what we came here for anyway. Keep looking for the files."

The girls carried on in comfortable silence. Saffron couldn't help her mind wandering repeatedly back to the photograph though. There was no doubt that was her father, Walter, as he existed right now was as he existed in that photograph, taken seventy years ago.

A violent shudder ran down her spine. She wanted to ask him about it but she couldn't do that without revealing what her and Mia had been doing in the first place. At the moment, Saffron felt her loyalties lay only with herself—she had to put herself before anyone else in order to survive the ordeal looming in her future.

"Got it!" Mia said, almost shouting in her excitement. "Look at this—the box is labelled 'Cropping Records'."

Saffron frowned. "What does that mean?"

Mia shrugged her shoulders. "I don't know. But

here—" she passed over a slender off yellow colour manila style folder to Saffron "—this is one of the files."

Saffron opened it. Several small photographs slid out of it, leaving behind a handful of sheets of paper. "Tammy Fischer," she murmured, flicking through the papers. "Born April 17th 1900."

"Wait, what?" Mia said, grabbing at the delicate papers. "She'll be the first one, the first offering!"

"What about Adala?"

"After her. Adala would have gone into the forest in 1900, so when Tammy turned seventeen, she was the first one to pay 'tribute' or whatever the hell it is."

"So that makes me number..." Saffron counted the years out on her fingers "...number seven?"

Mia nodded. "That's a lot of girls, isn't it? One every seventeen years doesn't sound so bad, but when you think Sehrstadt has existed since what...the late eighteen hundreds, and we've had six girls just disappear into the forest, under the pretence of some 'Offering' or whatever..." Mia shivered "...I dread to think what's happened to them."

Saffron flicked through the rest of the papers to find the death certificate, the last piece of delicate paper at the back of the file. "Date of death—September 21st 1934." Saffron shook her head. "How could they know this? If she went through the forest and was allowed out into the City, how could they know when she died?"

"Because she didn't make it to the City," Mia said. "She was in that forest for seventeen years, until the next Offering went in."

Saffron shook her head. "That's impossible. Nobody could live out there for all that time."

"Then why record the date of death as that?"

"Who deals with all these records?" Saffron asked.

Mia pursed her lips. "I don't know."

"Where are the other files?" Saffron said. "Let's check the others out."

The girls rummaged through the box, rifling through the precious remaining folders. Sure enough, exactly as Mia said, their dates of death were recorded as the date of the next Offering. All causes of death were listed as 'misadventure'.

"What the hell does that mean?" Saffron asked, frowning.

Mia didn't answer. She grabbed all the death certificates, looking at them each individually quickly in succession.

"Look at this!" she said, grabbing Saffron's forearm in excitement. "The handwriting on all the certificates is the same."

Saffron's heart stopped. "That's impossible."

"It's not," Mia replied. "Look."

The girls studied the handwriting very carefully, comparing each letter with careful scrutiny. Just as they decided that without doubt, all the certificates had in fact been written by the same hand, a strange sound came from the top of the staircase.

Both girls snapped their heads up, looking towards the door. A shadow moved along outside, its black edges blocking out the slivers of moonlight sneaking in underneath the door.

"Who is that?" Mia whispered. She picked up the flashlight and shone it towards the door.

"Don't!" Saffron hissed, snatching the item from her friend's hand. She placed it light down on the floor, very quietly. "They'll see it."

The shadow stopped moving, its opaque presence looming over the girl's exit. Minutes ticked by. Saffron's heart was in her throat, her pulse echoing through her ears. The shadow moved. Blurred edges became defined lines. A snuffling sound, like a dog sniffing, filtered down into the basement.

Saffron's blood ran cold. Fear exploded inside her in an instant. "It's here," she whispered, her voice trembling. "It's the wolf."

Mia's grip tightened. "What?"

A loud thud sounded against the door, followed by nails scraping down the wood. Mia shrieked, sending the creature into a frenzy. A paw pressed up against the bottom of the door, a long nail dug at the soft mud surface, sending dirt flying as it tried to dig its way under the secret entrance.

"Where's the exit to the hall?" Saffron whispered.

Mia shook her head. "It's...it's locked from the other side. Padlocked. Only Herr Schulz has the key."

Saffron pointed at the door blocked by the creature. "So that's our only way out?"

Mia nodded, choking on sobs of panic.

"Shhhh," Saffron said, trying her hardest not to show her fear.

Mia dug her nails into Saffron's forearm. Saffron winced and bit her lip, focusing on the pain rather than her sheer terror. She closed her eyes, willing the damn thing to go away, to leave her alone until it was time.

Minutes ticked by. Mud kept flying, nails kept scratching at the wood.

"Saffron," Mia whispered. "Look!"

Saffron opened her eyes to see a monstrous elongated snout poking through the hole under the door. Its nostrils flared as it inhaled the scents in the musty basement. A low growl emanated from the wolf.

Mia clamped a hand over her mouth, stifling her screams. Then the creature stilled. Seconds later it retreated, its thundering paws fading into the distance.

"Has it gone?" Mia whispered, her whole body shaking.

Saffron waited with bated breath. "I think so."

"I'm not going out there. No way. What if its waiting for us? What if it's ran off to lure us out?"

"I think you're giving it too much credit," Saffron replied. "It's just a wolf, Mia. It's not capable of thinking like that."

Saffron picked up the torch, illuminating the girl's world once more.

"They're a lot more intelligent than what you realise," Mia said. "I mean it. I'm not going out there."

"So what are you going to do then? Wait in here until Herr Schulz unlocks the other door in the morning?"

"Fine," Mia snapped. "But I'm not sticking my head out there first."

Saffron wished she'd made her knife already. She wished she even had something as simple as a hammer about her person, just something to swing at the beast in case it was lying in wait for them. Anything was better than nothing.

"Are we done with these files?" Saffron said, shining the torch on the open folders.

Mia nodded. "I just want to go home. We answered our questions, right?"

Saffron sighed. "I think I just have even more questions to be honest."

"But nothing that can be answered by staying down here."

"No. Let's tidy these away and go home."

The girl's worked in a quick, comfortable silence, carefully organising the files back to their original state. Once they were all packed away, Saffron stood up and held her hand out for Mia, offering her help to her feet.

"Come on," she said. "We'll be just fine. I promise."

Mia's face had drained to a ghostly white. She nodded, her lips pulled into a thin line.

Step by step, keeping the torchlight low, the girls ascended the creaky old stairs. Saffron kept her head low, using the freshly dug hole to scan across the grassy plain that waited for them outside. From her limited view, she could see nothing but short grass and the beginnings of the trees in the distance.

"I think we're all clear," she whispered to Mia, who was trailing behind her, clinging onto Saffron's forearm still.

"How do you know it's not hiding to the side or something?"

Saffron faced reality. "I don't."

Mia didn't reply.

When they reached the top of the staircase, Saffron prised her arm free from Mia. "I'm going to need both hands in case I have to shut the door again quickly."

Mia let go.

Easing the lock off, Saffron slowly slid the door open. Apprehension built inside her with each inch she dared to open the door. Her heart in her mouth, nausea churning in her stomach, she took a deep breath and braved looking outside.

The serene beauty of Sehrstadt's landscape stared back at her, bathed in moonlight. Not a single blade of glass moved across the wide-open space. The treeline seemed to call to her, almost laughing at her as it hid secrets she still had yet to discover, but nothing came for her this time.

"We're good," she said to Mia.

Quivering from head to toe, Mia clung to Saffron as Saffron exited the basement fully, standing clear at the back of the building.

"Lock the door up," she whispered to Mia.

Mia fumbled with the hidden latch, her fingers slipping.

"Take it easy," Saffron said. "Just breathe."

The lock slid into place. Mia grabbed Saffron's hand. Taking one cautionary step after another, the girls sidled along the side of the town hall, picking their way back home painfully slowly. When they eventually reached Mia's house, Saffron suddenly realised she had to get to her own house, alone.

"Are you going to be ok?" Mia asked, her eyes darting out across the sleeping town.

Saffron nodded. "I'll be ok, Mia. I'll talk to you tomorrow. Or later today, whichever."

Attempting to laugh, Saffron comforted herself with the prospect of being alone after such a fright. Even though her house was only a seven-minute walk from Mia's it suddenly seemed like a million miles.

Walking quickly but quietly, Saffron made it back to her house without further incident. Except for the persistent feeling of someone, or something, watching her from the treeline. As she closed her eyes to go to sleep, all she could see in her minds eye was an elongated snout and long claws coming for her under the door.

CHAPTER SEVENTEEN

After the close encounter in the basement, Saffron dare not suggest they go back down there to study the previous Offerings files further. She knew without doubt that Mia would say no, and deep down, Saffron didn't want to go back down there either.

School on Monday dragged by, but once it finally finished, Saffron headed to the forge as normal. When she ran past the town hall, she couldn't help but look at the secret back door, wondering if there would be any trace of the creature's presence left.

What she saw made her stop dead. The hole the wolf had dug out with its claws had been filled in, the earth smoothly compacted back down and fresh turf laid on top, as if nothing had ever disturbed the ground.

The deep scratch marks in the door no longer existed either.

Panic surged through Saffron's chest. She pressed a hand to her heart, trying to calm its raging rhythm. Someone knew. Someone knew that the wolf had been trying to get into the basement. And they'd covered it up. Not a word had been breathed around the town about this.

Fear coursed around her body. It was the defining moment of when Saffron knew she would truly be on her own as an Offering. Whatever was going on in this town, some of the adults clearly knew about it and were hiding its ominous presence.

Saffron tore her gaze from the secret door and forced herself to carry on to her father's forge. Every step she took, a fresh wave of despair washed over her. By the time she reached the forge, she felt like collapsing into a heap and just giving in to her fate.

Her father opened the door and stepped out for some air just in time to see Saffron doubled over, her head between her knees, gasping for breath.

"My goodness," he said, rushing to his daughter's side. "Are you ok, Saffron? I fear you're pushing yourself too far with all of this training."

Saffron felt like crying in relief but she fought back the tidal wave of tears. She knew once she started, she wouldn't stop.

"Yes, Papa," she said, lifting her head and giving her father a weak smile. "I'll be ok in a minute."

Saffron sat on the floor and lifted her face up to the bright blue sky as she drew in deep breaths. Her father stayed by her side until she calmed herself down enough to stop shaking and think rationally once more.

"Sorry, Papa," she said, staggering to her feet. "I pushed myself too far today."

"Come now, Saffron," he replied, helping his daughter to her feet. "Let's make a start on your knife. Give you a new focus, hmmm?"

Saffron couldn't help the grin that spread over her face. It was the exact thing she needed to renew her enthusiasm. She could beat this beast. If she didn't, she would sure as hell die trying.

As her father guided her in making her weapon, Saffron couldn't help but think that if she killed this wolf, she could at least bring her father some peace about what happened to his younger sister. The years of torment and guilt must have riddled him for years, Saffron thought to herself. She felt it was the least she could do to pay homage to her family.

Despite the heat around her, Saffron shuddered when she realised she was creating a weapon of death —something so beautiful that would be used in such an ugly way. Soon enough, it's perfect virgin surface would be tainted in hot, thick blood. Each drip falling from its serrated edge would only drive its hunger for more bloodshed.

As she moulded its very being, Saffron spoke to it, whispered her deepest, darkest thoughts and what it needed to do in order to protect her and save the next generation from such a hideous tradition. Each blow of the hammer formed its exquisite curves. Every red-hot patch glowed with her passion at ending this for those yet to be born. The individual teeth along its broad girth seemed to smile as she finished shaping each one with a tip so vicious, a samurai would be proud to carry it.

"That's enough for today, Saffron," her father said. "We can carry on working on it tomorrow. We have several weeks yet to perfect it."

Already attached to her beautiful blade, Saffron begrudgingly laid it down, silently telling it she would be back tomorrow to finish it.

CHAPTER EIGHTEEN

For the next two weeks, Saffron worked religiously on her blade. By the time she was done, she couldn't put the exquisite knife down. Its blood red coloured handle glistened under the light, the brass nails screwed into it for decoration gleamed with pride. The blade itself, long and curving, serrated on both sides, drove fear through her just at the sight of it. The damage it would cause to whatever lay in its path would be devastating.

Her father urged her to make a couple of smaller knives, weapons she could easily strap to her thigh or her ankle. Saffron didn't need telling twice. She jumped at the chance eagerly, relishing in the opportunity to create more lethal weapons.

Saffron passed on the chance to go on the next supply trip. Her and Mia had somewhat avoided one another since that frightful night, neither girl wanting to discuss it or revisit those terrifying moments again. The most interaction they'd had since was simply smiling at one another across the grassy plains.

Once Saffron had built herself a small arsenal of weapons, her father started teaching her how to wield them, how best to defend herself and also how best to attack.

"How do you know all this?" Saffron asked, thoroughly intrigued.

Walter hesitated for the smallest of moments before replying, "It's just things that have passed down through the family, from my father to me, from his father to him, and so on."

Saffron felt a huge sense of pride swell in her chest as she thought of family traditions and secrets being passed down from generation to generation, and now finally, she would be putting all of it to use, for real.

---

The days merged into weeks. Saffron quickly learned from her father and was now nothing but a formidable opponent for the monster that lay waiting for her within the forest. The Offering loomed on the horizon, the fateful day being only five days away.

As Saffron headed home from the forge that night,

twilight settling all around her, a familiar voice shouted her name from across the town square.

"Saffron!"

She turned around, surprised but somewhat relieved to see Mia rushing towards her. "Mia," Saffron said, holding her arms out for her friend. "It's so good to see you."

"You too."

The girls embraced each other quickly, then stood back.

"How have you been?" Mia asked.

"Good. I've made six weapons," Saffron whispered, scanning the immediate environment around her for potential eavesdroppers. "I'm ready. Papa has been teaching me how to fight."

"That's excellent. Listen, I was thinking about your weapons and about putting them out there before The Offering."

Saffron raised her eyebrows. "In the forest? You want to go into the forest after what happened?"

Mia shivered but nodded. "Your basket is going to be checked before you go out there. You can't hide them in there, and with the outfit too, you won't have anywhere to hide them. Putting them out there beforehand is the only way to make sure you've got them all."

"But I don't know where I'm going to be entering the forest."

Mia nodded. "I do. I've been back down in the archives doing some digging."

Saffron's mouth dropped wide open. "You went back down there?"

"Under the pretence of helping with some filing. I read through all of the Offering files. They all entered the forest at the same point."

"How do you know?"

Mia grinned. "The devil is in the details."

"Mia..."

"All the girls had their photographs taken before heading into the forest, right on the treeline. Every single one was taken near the same tree."

Saffron rolled her eyes. "Mia, how could you possibly know that? They're all the same."

"No, they're not. There's one tree, right on the border, that has a specific mark carved into it, way above head height, but it's there. You wouldn't notice it from the ground, walking around, but it's glaringly obvious in the pictures."

"What sort of mark?"

"I don't know how to explain it. I haven't got any paper on me to draw it either." Mia pursed her lips. "Meet me tomorrow and I'll show you a picture."

Saffron nodded. "Ok."

The girls arranged to meet at Saffron's paddock tomorrow evening at dusk. Saffron ran home, the anticipation of the coming days pulsing through her veins and driving her forwards. Her mind whirred with countless scenarios as to what would happen when she ventured into the forest for the final time.

She couldn't help but think that this time next week, she might not even be alive. Would this be her last Monday night ever? Saffron reached her house and opened the door. What greeted her in the kitchen made her rock back on her heels.

"Saffron," her mother said. "You're home just in time."

Her mother had cooked a feast fit for a King and laid it out on the kitchen table. Roast chicken, roast beef, bowls full of a variety of vegetables, freshly cooked bread, glasses of freshly squeezed orange juice...Saffron was truly astounded.

"What's all this?" she asked.

"We want to give you the best meals, the best food you ever tasted in this last week. Make sure you're as fit and strong as possible in the lead up to The Offering."

"That's lovely, Mama. Thank you so much."

"Don't be silly," Anna replied, ushering her daughter around the table to her seat. "You don't need to thank me for honouring my daughter."

"Mama," Saffron said, sitting in her seat. "You know I might not get chosen."

Anna stilled, only for the smallest of moments, but

it was noticeable enough. "I know that, but you could also *be* chosen. I would rather do this than not."

Saffron realised in that moment that without doubt, she would be chosen. All of the weapons she'd made, the training her father had given her, this week of farewell meals, this wasn't all hinged on a 'maybe'. Her parents knew something deeper about this than what they were letting on. The question was what.

CHAPTER NINETEEN

The next evening, just before dusk settled, Saffron slipped out to the paddock after a hearty meal that made her feel nothing but sleepy. Telling her parents she was checking on Hanna and Henry, she jogged down to the wooden fence, scanning over the landscape for Mia's petite form.

Saffron reached the gate, the two horses snuffling around a post a few feet to her right.

"Pssst."

Saffron spun around.

"Saffron," Mia whispered. "Down here."

Looking down, in front of where the horses were nuzzling the long grass under their fence, Saffron saw a dark green cloak, a few shades darker than the surrounding grass.

"Mia?"

"Shhhh. Don't look at me and talk. Pretend you're talking to the horses or something."

Saffron giggled. "What is this? Some sort of covert op?"

"If someone sees us, don't you think they're going to ask questions? Questions we can't answer right now."

"You mean two friends talking?"

"It's dusk, Saffron. You know the rules about being out after dark."

Saffron pursed her lips. Not being out after dark had been an unofficial law engrained in every child. With beasts such as the one they had already encountered on the prowl, Saffron was pretty certain that was why the rule existed.

Right on cue, Anna called out, "Saffron, it's nearly dark."

"Be right there, Mama," she shouted back.

"Here," Mia said.

Saffron looked down to see her friends pale fingers sliding a polaroid through the grass towards her feet. In the means of staying undercover, Saffron bent down and wrenched a handful of long grass with both hands, sneakily picking up the picture at the same time. Turning her back to her house, she offered the lush grass to the horses, sliding the small photo into her bra.

"Thanks," she whispered. "I'll come and find you tomorrow. We need to talk."

"My lunch break is at twelve. I'll be filing in the town hall again."

"See you then."

Saffron said goodnight to the horses and ran back to the house, trying not to worry about Mia being out after dark. Considering their close encounter weeks ago, Saffron couldn't help but admire her friend's bravery and courage to do such a thing, especially this close to the Offering.

When she went back inside her house, Saffron made an announcement to her parents.

"I think I'm going to take an evening ride after tea for the rest of the week," she said, trying to ignore the building lump in her throat. "After all, it could be my last chance to enjoy such a thing."

Walter and Anna looked at one another briefly before Anna replied, "Of course. We wouldn't deny you last minute pleasures, Saffron."

"I'm going to take a bath and head to bed. Thank you again for such a delicious tea, Mama."

Anna gave her daughter a beaming smile. Walter disappeared into the living room with his paper. Stepping in between her younger brother and two sisters fighting in the hallway, Saffron made it to the bathroom and locked the door behind her. Turning the taps on full blast, she whipped the picture from her bra and stared at it, looking for the mark Mia had told her about.

The beautiful young girl smiling in the picture made Saffron shudder. The hope shining from her brilliant blue eyes brought tears to Saffron's eyes. What fate she had suffered was unknown but Saffron knew for certain it was not pretty.

In the background, the treeline loomed like an ominous threat, a murky mix of dense greens and browns, waiting to swallow her forever. Over her left shoulder, a thick trunk, obscured by leafy low hanging branches, harboured a peculiar creamy coloured mark. Saffron squinted, trying to make out the shape.

Two rectangles stood upright, a small gap between them, with another rectangle laid across the top of them, like a crudely drawn thick set table. Saffron frowned. What the hell was that? And more importantly, who had put it there and why?

As the water started turning cold, Saffron realised she'd drained the hot water tank. She opened the door just enough to shout to her father that he would need to stoke the fire to heat the water up. Locking the door again, Saffron eased herself into the water, holding the picture in her hands. She sat and stared at it until the water turned tepid and her skin wrinkled like an old prune.

Something about the symbol provoked familiarity but she couldn't place where or why. An overwhelming sense of defeat prised Saffron out of the cold water. She cloaked herself in a fluffy white towel and retreated to her bedroom. As she walked into her room, her eyes fell to the bookshelf still harbouring all of her old books.

Then she remembered. She'd seen the symbol in Sehrstadt's history book, the one she'd been given when she turned thirteen. Rushing to her books, she pulled her town history book off the shelf and flicked through the pages. When she found the picture of Adala, beautifully painted in a scene spookily similar to the picture in her hand, Saffron gasped.

Behind Adala's left shoulder was a thick trunk, obscured by leafy low hanging branches. Painted on the tree trunk was the exact same symbol as what was in the picture. Saffron's mind ran wild. What did this mean? Had all these pictures been taken to replicate the history books or was this something more?

A violent shiver ran down Saffron's spine, telling her this was in fact, something much more. Saffron hid the stolen polaroid inside her history book and put it back on the shelf, just in case someone walked in. Drying herself, she contemplated her options here. There was no time, no more options to run back to the library for a book on symbols and meanings.

Saffron sighed and got ready for bed. She wondered what her younger brother and sisters would be told about her once she was gone. Tears sprung to her eyes. This time next week, she could potentially not even exist. Who would remember her? Life would go on without her, day after day as if she never even mattered. Her parents would eventually heal, and with her younger siblings to look after, their grief would be overshadowed.

Laying on her back, Saffron had a perfect view of the night sky out of her window. Stars twinkled above her, glittering gems against a black velvet background. The moon was almost full, its shining silver light beaming down to the ground, highlighting her bedroom in lunar shadows.

What felt like hours slid by until Saffron felt her eyelids drooping and her mind had exhausted itself from running wild with every possible scenario. She slipped into a deep sleep.

*Saffron found herself walking through the town square. The moon hung high in the sky, full and gleaming with beauty. With the fountain to her left, she headed right out of the square, slipping between the bakery and the butcher's. She headed towards the treeline, some unknown force compelling her forwards.*

*Her heart hammered in her chest. She whipped her head from side to side, scanning the landscape as her feet continued marching on. As she approached the trees, Saffron took one last look at the beautiful night sky above her and sucked in a deep breath. As she cast her eyes back down, they caught sight of a familiar mark on a familiar tree.*

*She froze. Every hair on her body stood up. Saffron shuddered and peered into the thick foliage, looking for a pair of glowing red eyes to be staring back at her. When she found nothing, she turned around to head back to the town square.*

*What faced her made her heart explode with adrenaline. The wolf, the very beast that had tried to dig its way to her and Mia in the basement, stood inches from her, staring at her. Its thick black nose was close enough for her to touch with barely a hand movement. Hot breath blew over her from its open mouth as its dark eyes bore holes into her soul.*

"*Gateway,*" *it said, taking a step forward.*

*Saffron took two steps back, her voice paralysed with fear.*

"*Gateway,*" *the creature repeated.*

"*Wh...what?*" *she breathed.*

*The wolf took another step, altering its course so it didn't tread on her. "Gateway."*

*It proceeded, very slowly, to head into the forest,*

*towards the tree with the mark on it. Saffron watched, dumbfounded, but her fear quickly disappearing. For some bizarre reason, she found herself following it past the marked tree, inside the forest.*

*As she passed the tree, she immediately noticed two more thick trunks marked with strange symbols, one either side of the worn path the beast was currently on. One symbol was a simple wavy line, the other a circle with several lines through it.*

*The wolf stopped and pointed its head to the right, looking up at the symbol of the wavy line. "Energy," it said. Then it looked at the other tree to the left and up at the circle and said, "Time."*

*Saffron frowned. Gateway, energy, time. What the hell did that mean?*

*The wolf stilled, its tail pointed out directly behind it. It lifted its nose into the air then let out a deep bellowing growl. Sheer terror poured into Saffron's body. This was it. She was going to die. A streak of orange dashed through the trees, followed by an almighty roar.*

*Saffron screamed...*


"Saffron, Saffron!"

Saffron jolted awake to see her mother leaning over her, shaking her gently. "Mama?"

"You were screaming," Anna said, wiping Saffron's sweaty forehead with a cold flannel. "Bad dream?"

Saffron nodded and sat up, her entire body shaking. "Can I have some water please?"

Anna smiled and lifted a fresh glass of water from the bedside table. "Expected you to ask," she said, smiling at her daughter.

"Thanks," Saffron replied, taking a grateful mouthful of refreshing water. "I'm ok, Mama. You can go back to bed."

"Are you sure?"

Saffron nodded and laid back down. "Yes, thank you."

"Ok." Anna bent down and kissed her daughter on the forehead. "See you in the morning."

Saffron smiled and rolled over, facing the wooden wall. Her mind had leapt into top gear, spinning with possibilities of meanings from her dream. After a while, fatigue won over and Saffron enjoyed a peaceful deep sleep.

CHAPTER TWENTY

When Saffron woke the next morning, she couldn't shake the dream from her mind. She was itching to head out to the treeline and investigate, see if there was in fact two more trees with strange marks.

By the time twelve o clock came around, she was nothing but a jittery bag of nerves as she waited to tell Mia about her latest nightmare and the mark from the history book.

"So it didn't try to attack you or anything?" Mia said, her forehead creasing in confusion. "That doesn't make any sense."

"I know," Saffron said. "I can't understand it. Do you think the words it said are what the symbols mean?"

Mia shrugged her shoulders. "I don't know. Possibly. What are we supposed to do with the information anyway? We can't decrypt three words and three weird marks."

"It must mean something, right? I've been having these dreams for months. They can't be a coincidence."

"I don't know, Saffron. I would like to think they mean something but the subconscious is a funny thing. It could just be your mind playing tricks on you."

Saffron shook her head. "Mama and Papa have been acting really strange this week. They've put on these really lavish feasts the past couple of nights, said they're going to do it every night. Apparently they want me well fed and my strength up before I go into the forest."

Mia frowned. "So? That's really nice. You are their eldest daughter, Saffron."

"No, you don't understand. It's like they *know* that I'm going to be chosen."

"I think you're over reacting, looking too much into it. They're just two parents scared of losing their child."

"Maybe. I just...I don't know...I've got this feeling that they know more. I can't explain it."

"It's Wednesday today," Mia said. "We need to plan getting your weapons into the forest."

Saffron nodded. "I've already told Mama and Papa

that I'm going riding every night now as a last minute pleasure. They're fine with it."

"Good. I'll meet you down by your paddock at five."

"Sounds good. I'll see you then. Oh," Saffron said, grinning. "Don't do the covert op thing again. I'll tell them you're coming with me."

Mia laughed. "I couldn't risk being caught with that photo. Sorry."

"Don't be sorry, it was interesting to say the least."

The girls parted company for the time being, both laughing to themselves about Mia's stealth act the night before.

Saffron spent the rest of the afternoon grooming the horses. Her father had left Hanna at home, leaving her fresh for Saffron's intended ride this evening. She'd just finished tacking up when Mia arrived, full of energy and her eyes bright and gleaming.

"Got your stuff?" Mia asked.

Saffron nodded and patted the saddle bag hanging from the back of the saddle. "I'm all good to go. You want to sit on Hanna with me?"

Mia widened her eyes and shook her head vehemently. "No. I prefer my feet to be on solid ground, thank you."

Saffron giggled and mounted up. "Could you open the gate then please, ground dweller?"

Mia laughed and opened the field gate. In comfortable silence, they made their way around the treeline, taking the long route to the area of the marked tree. By the time they reached the specific area, the town had fallen quiet, most people back in their homes, eating their evening meal.

Saffron pulled Hanna to a stop and dismounted. She untied the saddle bag and lead Hanna into the trees. Seeing no horse was better than seeing a horse without a rider. Several feet into the treeline, the girls found the tree from the pictures.

"This is so weird," Mia said, glancing around her nervously.

Saffron nodded. "It's eerie."

Under the thick foliage, sunlight barely penetrated through, casting the girls into a creepy shadow world of nothing but silence and ancient trees. The worn-down path the beast had stood on in her dream lay before them.

"There," Saffron said, pointing to the compacted earth. "That's the path."

Mia glanced towards where her friend was pointing. Darker shadows and denser foliage stared back at them both. "You want us to go that way?"

"Not far," Saffron said. "The other two trees, if they are in fact real, are just a few steps down."

Mia raised an eyebrow. "Lead the way then."

Saffron tightened her hand on Hanna's reins. If something was off or about to happen, the mare would react to it, alerting them both. It would be fine.

Taking a deep breath, Saffron clicked to Hanna and strode deeper into the trees, her eyes roving over the trees either side of the path, eagerly seeking out the pair of marked trees. Just as she said, several metres past the 'gateway' tree stood the two other trees.

"Here," Saffron said, staring at the strange symbols.

Mia hurried to her friend's side and looked at the trees. "This means something. I wasn't sure before but now I'm here, the atmosphere and everything else, this has a meaning, Saffron. We just need to figure out what."

Saffron nodded and held up her saddle bag full of her precious weapons. "Let's get these hidden and get back out before someone notices we're missing."

Pulling out a small hand trowel, Saffron indicated to Mia where to dig the hole and bury her saddle bag. Saffron kept an eye out, the treeline not far behind them. Minutes ticked by painfully.

"Done," Mia said, standing up and brushing the dirt off her dress and her hands. "Where can I put this?" she asked, holding up the hand trowel.

Saffron pointed to Hanna's other side where another saddle bag hung. "In there, please."

Mia nodded and obliged. The two girls emerged

from the forest sheepishly, their eyes darting around for any potential witnesses. Saffron quickly remounted Hanna and urged her forwards, continuing their ride around the forest border as if nothing had happened.

"It's getting dark," Mia said, her long legs easily keeping pace with Hanna's marching walk.

Saffron glanced up into the dusky sky, revelling in the pastel pinks and yellows blending together on the horizon. Would this be one of her last sunsets? She sighed and leaned down, wrapping her arms around Hanna's neck.

"What are you doing?" Mia said, a look of pure horror twisting her pretty face. "You'll fall off!"

Saffron giggled. "No, I won't. I'm just enjoying the moment. Cherishing the addictive smell of horses, the freedom of riding, the peace in my mind...a rare moment at this particular time in my life."

Mia pulled her lips into a thin line and gave her friend a pitiful smile. "I could probably hide out there somewhere, you know. Meet you in there, give you a hand."

Saffron shook her head. "I appreciate the offer, Mia, but I couldn't possibly let you do such a thing. I couldn't live with myself if anything happened to you because of me."

"I want to help."

"You have helped, more than you know. This is my

burden to bear, Mia. I'm not dragging you into it for the sake of it."

"If you change your mind, you only need ask."

Saffron smiled and nodded. "I won't but thank you."

The girls headed back towards Saffron's paddock, nothing but the sound of evening insects buzzing and the swish of Hanna's hooves brushing through the grass accompanying them. They parted ways with a small nod and smile, the evening's events successfully accomplished.

## CHAPTER TWENTY-ONE

Tomorrow was the Offering. An all-day celebration would take place before the Mayor chose the girl who would shoulder such an incredible responsibility. Just as twilight settled, the chosen youngster would be sent off into the forest on her 'special' journey.

After working late into the night, sharpening the blade on her knife, Saffron sat down with a sigh of satisfaction. She felt ready. Her heart beat strongly in her chest, her muscles had toned to become lean and strong over the past weeks, and her mind had naturally improved along with it. Confidence lay at the bottom of her foundations, urging her on.

She could do this.

And even if God himself damned her, she would do this.

The whole ridiculous show of the Offering day itself dragged by as if a tortoise itself was in charge of time. Saffron struggled not to show her contempt at the daft re-enactment some of the younger children played in front of the village. She barely managed a smile and gratitude as each business owner offered her something to carry in her basket: bread, meat, milk, fruit, vegetables, a leather pouch, a water canteen, and a beautiful forest-green blanket to keep her warm.

Saffron had made her own wicker basket, creating a false layer at the bottom. She didn't need much room for her deadly knife. Her other weaponry was already out in the forest, carefully hidden amongst the fallen leaves and damp earth.

Completely zoned out, Saffron paid no attention to Herr Schulz talking loudly until he said, "And so it is with great pleasure that this time around, this incredible honour has fallen on the shoulders of our very dear Saffron Schmidt."

Saffron froze when she heard her name. A swell of nausea rolled in her stomach. She knew this was her fate but somehow, the fact it hadn't been sealed yet gave her the tiniest sliver of hope that she might in fact see next week. Now Herr Schulz had declared she was about to die, a tsunami of panic hit her full force, pinning her to her seat.

"Saffron," Herr Schulz said, his round face beaming with pride. "Come here, dear. Let's get you ready. The sun isn't far from setting."

The other six girls surrounding Saffron clapped relentlessly, their eyes swimming with tears and their smiles too broad to be genuine. *If only they knew,* Saffron thought to herself.

Walter and Anna rushed up on stage to hug their daughter goodbye. The heat from her mother's tears still warmed her cheek as she was taken to the marked tree, to the 'gateway.'

"Saffron Schmidt, it has been an honour having you in our community. May your life be full of the fruits of love and joy," Herr Schulz said, ushering her towards the treeline.

Saffron swallowed the lump in her throat. She suddenly felt very alone, very vulnerable, and very small. As the last of the suns rays disappeared overhead, Saffron pulled up the hood on her red riding cape, and turned to beam at the camera. The click of the shutter became lost to a sea of cheers and applause. The cool September breeze skimmed across her bare legs, covering her in goose bumps.

But Saffron refused to give in to the shudder wanting to take control of her. Tonight, every natural instinct within her would have to be ignored, or by morning, she would be dead.

Saffron choked back the dawning horror of her immortalised picture now being in the history books. An identical one to the painted image in her history book and the polaroid images of all the previous Offerings. From this moment on, she would be nothing more than a mere picture in some archive filing of the community records.

Turning her back on her people, Saffron held her head high, squared her shoulders, and marched into the treeline. She darted behind the marked pair of trees, retrieving her weapons. Picking out one device in particular, Saffron picked her way through the forest, looking for the trail her father had described to her in great detail—the trail he and his sister had been on when they encountered the creature.

Saffron decided the same trail would be a safe bet for the beast to use again. Off the main hunter tracks, it provided perfect coverage from being seen but also allowed the ideal view of anything along the main trail. It tailed off into overgrown shrubbery, disappearing further inside a dense copse of trees.

Following tracks on it, it was obvious that deer used it often. If deer were part of this thing's diet, this would be a hot point of activity—a quick strike at the prey before dragging it back inside the cover of trees.

If Saffron's calculations were correct and the memories of her father untarnished, the unknown monster would be showing itself within minutes of the night falling. Looking up at the darkening sky above her, Saffron estimated roughly an hour, maximum, before her fate was sealed.

Going back to the village would be a fruitless effort. No one would take her seriously, except those in the know, and those who did know would force her back out to the forest to keep the peace inside Sehrstadt.

What puzzled Saffron was exactly how this whole thing had come about. Why did it only come back every seventeen years? And why did it have to be a seventeen-year-old girl with blonde hair and blue eyes, dressed up in a little uniform like she was being paraded around for a group of paedophiles?

She glanced into the shadowy forest ahead of her and hopped across the trails, setting her course for the beginning of her night. Laying her trap carefully and quickly, she retreated back under cover and waited.

Within minutes, an arrow of fear struck her heart.

She heard it before she saw it.

The ground beneath her shook as if a giant itself galloped towards her. Its thudding rhythm never faltered. Even from where she stood, pressed between the smallest of gaps between two old trees, the snapping of its jaws echoed around the silent night.

*How could people in the village not hear this?* she thought, amazed and frightened of the coming moments.

Bushes rustled, branches cracked, and leaves fell around her like ominous confetti, showering her with death. Then suddenly, as if someone had pressed pause, came utter silence. Saffron held her breath and squeezed her eyes shut. A deep, menacing growl vibrated through the chilly air, shaking every cell within her.

Within seconds, the thundering run continued. Every quake beneath her leather plimsoles became stronger, reaffirming this beast was heading straight for her.

*Five, four, three...*

A snap of metal came before a clunk. So instantaneous, the sound of success was very nearly lost to the frustrated howl of agony wailing from the beast's mouth. Saffron dared to release her breath. Having not realised how long she'd been holding it for, she gasped for air as she realised her bear trap had worked. She'd caught the beast. The creature that mutilated her father and took her aunt before she ever even knew her. Singlehandedly, Saffron had taken down a monster that had taken so many lives for too many years.

But she didn't realise her desperate inhale for air had been too loud. The screams of pain from the beast turned into barks of determination. She resisted the urge to whimper and clamped a hand over her mouth. She bent down and settled her basket on the forest floor as silently as possible. When the next angry shout sounded from the creature, she dug a path through the basket and grasped a hold on the small ribbon that would open the hatch to the false layer. Two growls later and her knife was in her hand.

Then she heard the most terrifying sound she would ever hear in her life—the light metallic ping of metal chains breaking. Saffron squeezed her eyes shut. Instead of its flat-out gallop, a heavy, three-thud walk dragged itself towards her.

*Please, please, please work. If there is anyone or anything in this universe listening to me right now, please make this work!*

The snap of a rope blessed her ears. Behind her, within twenty feet, the groan of a thick tree branch stole all attention. Two seconds later, she heard a deafening hollow thud, the wheeze of air being forced from lungs, and finally, the combined sound of more metal snapping and a high-pitched squeal.

Realising her legs were shaking, the thought to give in and collapse on the cold earth was almost as tempting as ice cream on a summer's day. Saffron kept her focus, ignoring her aching legs. She needed to wait for this thing to tire itself out. There was no way she would beat the beast in a contest of speed or strength. The only thing she had as an advantage was the fact she knew it existed in the first place. All of her cards had now been played. Now it was just her and the beast.

Seconds later, a chilling snarl echoed through the trees. Saffron froze. The thudding of her heartbeat almost deafened her. Rustling leaves sounded around her followed by the snapping of fallen branches. An angry growl vibrated through the darkness. More rustling. A louder snarl. The clack of teeth as a jaw opened and closed furiously. This cycle continued for a long time, long enough for Saffron to miss the gentle tickle of a spider climbing her leg. Saffron didn't care. The sly smile dominating her pretty face hid the icy fear pumping through her body. When the rustle of leaves stopped, all that remained was the heavy, laboured breaths of an exhausted creature.

Saffron closed her eyes and took a deep breath. This was it—do or die.

CHAPTER TWENTY-TWO

Saffron gripped the knife in her hand, reminding herself it was there. She couldn't believe how perfectly it nestled in her palm, so comfortable, silent, and lethal. The edge of the blade glinted under the moonlight, reflecting off the dark tree trunks around her. The heavy breathing in front of her shallowed. A grunt replaced exertion. She knew it had sensed her presence. A smirk of triumph twitched at her lips. This thing would finally be getting a taste of its own medicine. The pain it adored inflicting on others would now be turned on it.

Saffron didn't care if she died tonight. This ended here. Now.

Seeing the moon high in the sky above her, she took a moment to revel in the beauty of a clear night in the forest. A shiver of fear ran down her spine. Now was the time to see what it was, to face reality, and to take the life of another living being.

She stepped into the clearing, holding her right arm across her chest with her knife tucked back against her forearm. Under the glaring lunar light, a mound of dark, shaggy fur moved up and down with rapid breathing. Spirals of steam misted into the air around it, highlighting its sweat-soaked body.

Saffron took care to keep the chunky log that had knocked it off its feet in between them. Within a foot of reaching the felled tree, the beast snapped its head up and looked right at her. Two beady black eyes as dark as coal glared back at her, hatred oozing from their depths. It curled its top lip back into a frightening snarl.

As she stood there looking at it, taking in its long snout, powerful jaws, and its massive muscled body, the truth of what it was shocked her to the core. Seeing it in the flesh was so much more astounding than when she had encountered it in her dreams.

The wolf flopped its head back onto the dark ground. A strange noise emanated from it, that if she didn't know better, sounded like laughter. *Human* laughter. This couldn't be real.

"A werewolf?" she whispered to herself. "A werewolf?"

These things were of legends, myths, creepy tales told around a campfire on a blustery winter's night, not real stories. This couldn't be real. Maybe she was already dead, and this was her own vision of what she thought was happening.

Ice pooled in her feet. Fear stilled her heart. Panic left her blank of any sort of plan she had had of what would happen next. By now, she should have slit its throat and be carving out its oversized heart to take back to the village in a victorious act.

She reminded herself that werewolves were human. In daylight, this beast wouldn't exist, but in its place, a man would. The fact it could laugh alerted her to a distinct possibility—the myth of blind rage and an insatiable lust for blood overwhelming any humanity is a lie. In wolf form, these monsters are supposed to be as dumb as they are strong.

This one clearly wasn't.

Now came the problem of what to do next.

Daring to take a step closer, Saffron cleared her throat. "Can...can you...understand me?"

She felt foolish talking to a creature, a beast of myths and legends. Maybe she'd heard wrong, and it wasn't human laughter, or maybe it was just some kind of painful noise and a coincidence it happened after she spoke.

The wolf moved its head, too tired to even lift it. In

a strange moment of reiteration, the up-and-down movement it made in the form of a nod took Saffron's breath away.

*Now what?* she thought.

It had basic comprehension which completely took away the burning anger inside her. Being knocked off track was one thing she hadn't accounted for. In the midst of a fight, to stab something and steal its right to live was one thing, but to do so when it was incapacitated and clearly willing to communicate was quite something else.

Plus, the question of what exactly had happened to all the girls still needed an answer. Squeezing the knife in her right hand, she reminded herself that's what this was for, to get answers. Behind a newfound wave of confidence, Saffron sat on the log and stared at her captured prey.

"I have questions," she said, twizzling the knife between her fingers. "Are you going to answer them for me?"

The same head movement from a moment ago indicated its positive answer.

"Can you speak?"

It moved one of its huge front legs towards her. Saffron watched in confusion as it extended its paw as far as possible, only several inches from actually touching her. She fought the urge to move back, to scuttle away from the potential danger that a paw the size of her head could inflict.

Saffron asked her question again, only to frown when the beast moved its leg back a few inches and then re-extended it towards her. It made this movement several times before Saffron found a viable question.

"Me?" she asked.

The beast nodded.

"What about me?"

Nothing.

*Okay,* she thought. *Obviously this thing works like a Ouija board—yes or no only.*

"So you can speak, and it's got something to do with me?"

The beast offered another nod but less movement.

It was then that Saffron noticed a pool of blood forming underneath its injured leg. With the vicious metal clamp still locked around its prize like jaws of death, the wounds were unable to heal like before, when her father had speared it all those years ago.

Frowning, Saffron pursed her lips. "Me directly? Or just me as a person?"

Again, the wolf moved its leg slightly back and then forwards several times, seemingly pointing at her.

"As a person?"

It gave another nod but a faint one. The beast blinked, but it took several seconds for its eyes to reopen.

A light bulb went on in Saffron's head. "You can only speak as a person?"

The creature nodded and sighed.

Remembering the old legends, Saffron became frustrated. This would mean having to wait until daylight for the wolf to turn back into a man. A stroke of embarrassment caught her heart.

*He'll be naked*, she thought.

"Daylight is hours away yet. I can't let you go until then. You do understand that, right?"

The wolf lifted his head and shook it vehemently.

Saffron stood and stepped back over the log, suddenly fearing the creature she had sympathised with. "I will hurt you if I have to."

A deep growl vibrated from its body. It curled its top lip back and stared at Saffron as if trying to rip her apart already. In a move she never expected, the beast leapt to its feet, visibly pulsing with energy. It held its trapped front leg above the ground, all the time glaring at Saffron.

Seeing the horse-sized monster stood in front of her, Saffron debated her best option for going in for a strike. With it favouring its nearside paw, using that open area would be the ideal advantage. Plus, she would be close enough to inflict more pain if necessary.

The wolf's growl grew louder. It drew back its top lip completely, revealing nothing but razor-sharp teeth and two heart-stopping-sized canines. As if to highlight its lethality, the beam of moonlight guiding her glinted off the pointed tips, almost beckoning her to test their severity.

Saffron stepped back over the log, squared her shoulders, and commanded her harshest voice. "You know what? Fuck you!"

Not even thinking of any plan of attack, Saffron threw herself at the wolf, determined to hurt it as she'd originally intended. She aimed for her bear trap which would give her something other than the beast to hang on to.

In one swift motion, just as she'd been shown by her father, she sliced along its foreleg and followed the movement out, running towards its chest. She grasped her knife with both hands and lifted it above her head, ready to plunge it in the beast's chest.

The wolf shot forwards. With enough range left on the chain of the bear trap, the wolf hit Saffron in the head with the metal vice. The heavy, dull thud echoed through the forest. As she fell to the ground, the wolf hit her legs with the trap, sending her spinning across the dirt and loose earth.

With agony bursting inside her skull, Saffron fought to stay awake as long as she could. As the shadows closed in around her, the last thing she saw was the heaving underbelly of the beast and its jet-black eyes staring at her from between its front legs.

## CHAPTER TWENTY-THREE

Saffron fluttered her eyelids open. Darkness surrounded her with the faint glow of a flickering orange light coming from her left. The pounding inside her head made her cringe. Her legs shouted in pain, and every part of her body moaned with a heavy ache.

She moved her neck from side to side, attempting to free off some stiffness, but instead all she did was groan at the unexpected fight her joints put up against her.

"Well, hello, dear girl. I didn't expect you awake just yet." The soft, warm voice of an old lady floated over her, lulling her into a comfortable trance of semi consciousness and exhaustion.

Looking above her, Saffron noticed the diagonal slant of a roof made of logs peaking to its point. Something in the far recesses of her memory waved flags at her in desperation.

"How are you feeling? Would you like some tea perhaps?"

Saffron licked her lips, and at realising the dryness of her raw throat, managed to croak. "Please."

"Coming right up, dear girl. I'll get the old teapot on the stove and help you sit up."

The fog in Saffron's brain wouldn't clear. Despite how much she tried to fight through it, it swirled around her even more, leaving her with just enough consciousness for basic function. Gasping at the effort to try to remember something, anything, her father's face appeared from her memories.

"My father," Saffron whispered. "Papa was here."

The old lady returned, humming a lullaby from old times. "You can call me Addie, dear girl. Now, let me help you sit up."

Almost like a zombie, Saffron could do nothing as Addie turned the table she was on ninety degrees and then hoisted her into a sitting position with her back leaning against the wall. Entranced by the open fire, Saffron couldn't help but stare into it like a moth drawn to light. The dancing yellow-and-orange flames were so pretty, so alive, and yet so...controlled.

When she noticed what lay in front of it, she

choked in fear. Her eyes widened to the point of pain, but her body still refused to move.

"Oh, don't worry about him, dear," Addie said, waving a hand at the beautifully lethal tiger preening itself. "He's a big old softie. Hard to get him to do anything these days, except when it comes to chasing dogs. He just can't get enough of them."

Puzzle pieces clicked together in the back of Saffron's mind, but she still couldn't fight a clear path through the haze. The beauty of the beast amazed her as much as it frightened her. How could something so alive and wild be so tame inside such a small space? Saffron pondered over this as she watched the feline lie on its side and bask its belly in the heat.

Addie placed a cool, wrinkled hand against Saffron's forehead and smiled. Saffron managed to snap her eyes from the big cat and look at the lady in front of her. She had vibrant-blue eyes, pink, crinkled lips, a small button nose, and blonde, curly hair that had started growing dark roots. The smile pushing up both cheeks was inviting and relaxed Saffron into a state of ease.

"You haven't even suffered any shock yet," Addie said, taking her hand back. "You are a strong one."

Drowsiness threatened to pull Saffron back into a dark sleep. She was so tired; she could sleep for a decade. When her eyelids started to droop, she struggled to lift them open.

"Now, now, dear girl. You can't sleep just yet. We need to keep your strength up, and that"—the whistling of the teapot cut through the small cabin—"means plenty of fluids and food."

Leaning back against the wall of the log cabin was not a comfortable experience. Saffron inched herself in several directions, trying to alleviate some pressure from her spine. She glanced down and noticed a comfortable forest-green blanket covering her from the waist downwards.

She lifted her left hand and, with a heavy exhale, managed to grab the blanket. After counting to three in her head, she sucked in a deep breath and pulled it off her. Her legs screamed in pain, and after a second, Saffron moved her eyes to look at them.

It took quite a few moments for her brain to register what her eyes were seeing, then a few more moments for the urgency of that image to reach the right parts of her brain. Finally, after a good ten seconds or more, Saffron became consciously aware of her dire situation.

No wonder her legs were shrieking in agony. Both were missing flesh from the shins. Nothing at all covered the tops of her ankles to the bottom of her knees. All that stared back at her was a sickening mess of blood, bone, and muscle.

A surge of nausea rolled around in her stomach. She glanced at the old lady humming away as she poured two cups of tea. Saffron pushed back the thinning fog in her mind. Thirst was almost killing her, but her basic instincts told her not to touch the tea.

Still not of quite enough mind to even debate what the hell to do next, she had no choice but to sit there and wait for her hazy mind to clear itself.

Addie turned around with the two drinks. The instant she saw Saffron's blanket in her hand and baring her legs, she jumped, dropping the fragile cups. The huge cat barely twitched an ear.

"My goodness," she said, rushing forwards. "You weren't supposed to know of this just yet. I'm so sorry."

The woman grabbed the blanket from Saffron's hand, but Saffron refused to let go. "What is this?" she gasped.

Addie tutted, sighed, and let go of the blanket. "Well, I may as well tell you. No amount of valerian root is going to override this little memory." The woman sighed and walked back to where she'd dropped the china teacups. "It takes a lot, you know, to remain alive all these years. And a lot more still to retain youthful good looks. Everything in life that you want, whether it be a baby or a good job, requires some sort of sacrifice. I happen to want immortality and beauty. That requires a sacrifice." She bent down to retrieve the broken pieces of china. When she stood back up, she looked straight at Saffron and said, "Unfortunately for you, dear girl, you are that sacrifice."

Rising panic started to balloon inside Saffron. The fog in her mind was clearing by the second. She watched the old lady walk towards the small door that led outside. After carefully placing the broken cups on what Saffron assumed was the ground, she closed the door and leaned back against it.

"I imagine by now that your mind is almost clear. Am I right?"

Saffron nodded, swallowing the ball of fear in her throat.

"All you had to do was drink the tea," Addie said, her voice rising in irritation the more she spoke. "But even that's too much for you youngsters these days, isn't it? Just can't do as you're damn well told. That was all you had to do, dear girl. I'm not supposed to have favourites, but if I did, I have to admit you'd be it."

*Dear girl*, Saffron thought, chasing away the last of the mind fog. *That's what Father calls me. Why is she using it too?*

"Do you know," Addie said, continuing. "It took me three days to induce you into your pain-free, semi-conscious state? It takes quite a knowledge of botany and biology to have such skills you know."

"My father," Saffron said, clearing her throat. "My father was here once."

Addie chuckled. "My dear girl, your father has been here more than once." Laughing to herself, the woman took an old tea towel and wiped the liquid on the floor. "Your father was born here, sweetheart. One never forgets their way back to their mother."

Saffron gasped. "That means you're my...you're my—"

"Grand-ma-ma," Addie replied, standing back up. "Yes, I am your granny, Saffron, but I'm afraid that's as close as our connection gets." She threw the tea towel into the fire, letting the hiss of the damp material fill the silence for a moment. "Because call me selfish if you want to, but having immortal beauty is of far more importance to me than anything else. As you can see, I'm still chasing away the last of old age after finishing the last girl a little too early. I should have started on your thighs to give me the best boost, but you had such bad bruising on your shins, I needed to get that before it soured any further."

Without realising it, tears trickled down Saffron's pale face. She couldn't quite grasp the scale of what was being told to her. Her mind raced, trying to picture together everything she'd ever been told. She and the previous girls were a sacrifice for a witch to have immortality and beauty? What the hell?

"I...I...I don't understand..."

Addie prodded the tiger to move, sticking her fingers beneath it to retrieve a piece of the broken porcelain. "It's quite simple really, dear girl. In order to keep me alive and forever beautiful, I need to consume my own flesh and blood. I don't need much, just a mouthful a day. By the time I'm finished with you, the next girl will be here. And so on."

Saffron choked on her sobs, fighting herself not to look at the gruesome mess her legs were currently in. Her head throbbed with such an overwhelming turn of events.

"If you're worried about the pain, sweetheart, don't be. I'm quite the expert nowadays. The last girl managed to stay alive right up until I had nothing left but her vital organs. She was quite a talker actually, lovely girl."

"No," she said, shaking her head. "No. This isn't right. Father... Papa loves me. He trained me, helped me, told me things...the wolf. Are you the wolf?"

Addie cackled like a wicked witch. "Dear girl, no. I'm a witch not a brute of a dog. That damn creature has been the bane of our lives. We never have managed to figure out who that is—yet. The miserable little sod, whoever they are, knows of us and our needed...

patterns. He wasn't trying to eat you, my dear girl, he was trying to save you."

More tears fell down Saffron's cheeks. "So father was...was teachi—"

"Teaching you how to kill it. Yes. We've both failed numerous times. I thought Aslan would be able to take it down, but, as you can see—"she motioned a hand towards the snoring tiger "—that's not quite worked out either."

Saffron couldn't help but screw her face up in shock and disgust at the woman. What was wrong with her? This had to be a bad dream. It just had to be.

"I know what you're thinking," Addie said, turning her attention to the oven. "He's not a lion—I know—but lions don't tend to favour canine meat like tigers. Plus, if you hadn't noticed"—she opened her arms with her blackened oven gloves on— "I don't have a wardrobe either." The old woman cackled. "The tiger, the witch, and the log cabin."

*What the...? This woman has got to be on drugs, surely? I need to get out. Please, if anyone in the universe is listening right now, please help me!*

Saffron closed her eyes, trying to block out her visual reality as much as possible. Thinking back to the wolf, she remembered being under its belly with it looking at her from between its front legs. It had stood over her to protect her, not hurt her. She felt so foolish.

And she'd hurt this blessed monster based on the lies she'd been fed. Anger boiled inside her. She wanted to scream, shout, hurt this thing in front of her, make it bleed, make it suffer.

But any twinge she indicated to her body crippled her with agony at the reminder of her legs.

"Anyway," Addie said, pulling something out of the oven. "Seeing as you're fully conscious and more than aware of what's going on around you, I guess there's no point in Grand-ma-ma's special home-brew tea anymore." She removed her oven gloves, crossed her arms over her chest, and rested an index finger on her chin, deep in thought. "You know, I've never actually tried savouring one of you without you being drugged. I've heard it makes the muscle more tender, with the flow of adrenaline and all. I guess I owe you a thank-you for allowing me the opportunity to taste something I've always wondered about." She waved a hand over herself. "As you can see, I can't really afford to wait three days again for the drugs to take effect. Not after I finished What's Her Name a week too early."

"You're a sick, sick lady," Saffron replied, spitting out her words. "Do you not care about all the families you've hurt by taking their children from them? Do you not have one ounce of sympathy at all? What would you do if someone did this to—" she paused, not wanting to use the name 'Papa' "—Walter, hmmm?"

"All the families? My dear girl, they merely grieved for a daughter they thought was theirs. Well, the men anyway. Every sacrifice has been sired by your father, sweetheart. They have to be, or this wouldn't work."

"What?" Saffron said, choking on her words. "They've all been my sisters?"

"Well, yes. I can't just consume any virgin youth. That would be silly. The sacrifice has to be my own flesh and blood. Hence, you."

Saffron thought of the other girls who had competed for this special 'honour'. Were they her sisters or genuine children from other families? None of that mattered anyway. She knew for a fact none of them were virgins.

"They have to be virgins?"

Addie snorted. "Of course. Have you ever tasted the flesh of someone who has been diseased with lust and sexual pleasure?" The woman shivered and wrinkled her nose in disgust. "Makes me want to vomit. Disgusting stuff."

"But...but...what about Mama? Does she know?"

Addie threw her head back and laughed. "Of course she does. What woman do you know could bear four children and still look that good? Why do you think we wanted her as our main battery hen? There's something about the combination of her and your father that makes you taste so delicious. I've made it very clear that I want no other source now other than him and Anna. That's why Helga had to go."

"Helga?"

"His beloved little sister. I couldn't let her breed and have my vitality source running all over the place. That's for me and me only. Well, except for what I have to gift to your father and mother to keep them going. Helga wouldn't let me sterilise her, so I ate her." She shrugged her shoulders with such a nonchalant move, it made Saffron feel sick.

"What about the rest of the village?" Saffron asked, curious how they fitted in. "The ones that aren't...you."

"Oh, they're just a perfect cover." Addie waved her hand through the air. She turned her back and started rummaging through a drawer. "Where did I put my steak knife?" she muttered to herself.

Lost in her own thoughts, Saffron couldn't grasp this situation at all. She thought back to little Klaus and his curly blond hair, his grubby little hands constantly covered in mud and parts of worms and always tugging on her best dresses, making them filthy.

Saffron closed her eyes and sighed. *Suck it up, buttercup.*

CHAPTER TWENTY-FOUR

Saffron woke with a jolt. She looked around her to see she was still in the wretched cabin in the woods, but it was empty. The door was wide open, letting in a cool breeze that drafted over the dying fire. On top of the stove sat a clear dish full of what looked like pie. When she looked at her legs, her stomach churned at the thought of what was in that damned pie.

"Hello?" she called out, feeling rather unnerved at the sudden abandonment. Was this some sort of screwed-up test she had to somehow figure out, or had she genuinely been left alone?

The tiger had disappeared too. Was it going to come back and attack her? Was this some sort of adrenaline-inducing game Addie wanted to 'flavour' her meat?

Saffron shivered at the thought whilst still struggling with reality. She knew she needed to move, needed to leave. Help would be miles away, but it definitely wouldn't be any closer if she stayed in here.

Noticing the blanket still in her hand, she looked around her for something to cut it with. She soon spotted an axe hanging by the door. It was only a matter of twenty feet or so, but it may as well have been fifty miles. The instant she moved a leg, roaring agony caused her to cry out in pain.

Determined to move, Saffron took a deep breath and swung her legs off the side of the table. *There is no pain. There is no pain*, was the only thought she allowed to dominate her mind. Unfortunately, when she attempted to stand, her legs couldn't bear the strain. She collapsed on the floor in a crumpled, sobbing mess.

Heavy thudding sounded from outside, becoming louder and louder by the second. Completely vulnerable and with nothing to defend herself with, Saffron didn't even bother trying to hide. Through the open door, a man ran in, tall, broad, and pulsing with muscle. From his bulging arms straining against his red-and-black-checked shirt, mud-covered jeans, and heavy rigger boots,

Saffron recognised him immediately as a lumberjack. Then her brain kicked in and she realised he was the man from her dreams. How was this possible? Not caring how he got there, bearing in mind the only known loggers were well over twenty miles away, she cried in relief.

"Please help me. Please."

"Oh, dear God," he said, his husky voice only adding to the masculine image before her.

He rushed over, reached behind him, and pulled Saffron's knife from his belt. He took the forest-green blanket from her hand and shredded the soft material into two halves.

"Beautiful knife, this," he said, winking at her. "Could probably even kill a wolf."

Saffron sucked in a breath. "You're the wolf?"

"Alrik Baumhauer, Miss Saffron."

"You know my name?"

Alrik carefully laid one of the halves flat on the floor. From inside his shirt, he pulled out a strange, weaved sheet of plant leaves. With no explanation at all, he wrapped it around her exposed muscle and bone.

Saffron held her breath, waiting for the explosion of excruciating pain. But all that followed was the gentle soothing of cool gel against burning tissue. To keep it in place, Alrik wrapped one half of the blanket over the sheet of plants, tying an exuberant knot to keep it secure. He repeated the process with her other leg and then gave her a dazzling smile.

"Of course I know your name. It is my business to know all about those whom I attempt to save." He scooped her up and carried her outside. "You are my first success. Congratulations."

Saffron managed a small laugh. "I'm so sorry. My Pap—Walter had told me—"

"It's okay," he said. "I understand."

The clumping of boots on the wooden porch outside alerted Saffron to another presence. "Have you got her?" said a familiar male voice.

Saffron stared at the open doorway, then when the familiar face of Sam, the librarian, appeared, she gasped. "Sam? What are you doing here?"

He grinned at her. "It's a long story. I'm here to help, Saffron. You don't need to fear me."

"I'm not going anywhere," she said, smirking. "Indulge me."

The two men carefully lifted Saffron back onto the table. Alrik plumped the remainder of the blanket into a pillow and gently tilted Saffron's head up to place it underneath.

"I'm a witch," Sam said.

Every muscle in Saffron's body immediately tensed. Her hands clenched into fists as fear poured into her in fresh droves.

"Of the good kind," Sam said, chuckling. "Adala has been somewhat of a curse to our kind for many centuries. We have been trying to stop her for a long time, but her magic has always been too powerful. I hate to admit it, but she's a clever bitch."

"What made this time different?"

Sam held his hands out over her left leg, hovering them a few inches above her mutilated shin. "One, she killed the previous girl early so her powers are weaker than normal. Two, you."

"Saffron!"

Saffron looked to her left to see Mia running through the door. "Mia? What...what?"

Mia ran to her friend and threw her arms around her neck. "I'm so pleased you're alive."

Tears fell freely from Saffron as she embraced her friend fully, thankful to enjoy such a simple moment. "What are you doing here?"

Mia blushed and glanced at Sam. "Sam and I are kind of a thing...he's been helping us from the outside."

"I wish you'd read those books I loaned you," Sam said, grinning. "You might have realised sooner that the beast was a werewolf."

"When it was trying to claw its way through a door to eat us?" Saffron said. "No way."

Alrik took hold of Saffron's hand and said, "I was desperate to get to you and tell you, warn you, of what was coming. The only way I could reach you in the end was through Sam's magic in your dreams."

"The symbols..." Saffron said. "You knew what the symbols meant?"

Alrik nodded. "This is Adala's domain. A domain where endless energy means endless time—"

"And I entered the gateway to it." Saffron sighed. "It seems so simple now."

"Don't beat yourself up," he whispered. "The main thing is you're alive."

"What was the deal with the tiger?"

Alrik shuddered. "Tigers are the only thing that can kill werewolves. They relish in our flesh. Of course, once Adala knew I was hunting her, the best way for her to protect herself was with a tiger."

"That's why it was always in my dreams. It was hunting you, not me."

He nodded. "Unfortunately, the distance between Sam's magic and you was so great, the dreams became distorted, not quite as clear as I wanted them to be."

A fuzzy warm feeling from her left leg stole Saffron's attention. Pins and needles danced up and down the left-hand side of her body.

"What are you doing?" she asked Sam.

Sam had his eyes closed and his lips were moving quickly, whispering words Saffron didn't recognise.

"He's healing your leg," Mia said, squeezing Saffron's free hand.

"But it has no skin."

"He's a witch, Saffron," Mia replied, giggling.

"I didn't realise that meant re-growing skin."

"Well now you do."

The two girls grinned at each other like school children. Several long minutes passed, then Sam fluttered his eyes open and smiled at Saffron.

"Shall we have a look?" he said.

Saffron's heart back flipped. Had he really just healed her wound? She nodded. Sam carefully peeled back the blanket, then removed the soothing leaf. When soft smooth skin stared back at her, Saffron gasped and cried tears of joy.

"Thank you so much." She swallowed the lump in her throat and then said, "Where...where is she?"

"Adala has been taken back to the village. Walter and Anna have been captured and arrested," Mia said, a look of sorrow crossing her pretty features. "We're going to take you back as proof, a living witness to the horrors that have happened."

Saffron nodded and sat up. "Let's go."

"Wait," Sam said, pointing to her right leg. "You're not fully healed."

"They're not going to believe me if I walk back in there without a mark on me."

Alrik and Sam shared a worried look. "You want to go back with your leg so damaged?" Alrik asked.

She nodded. "Sam can heal it once it's served its purpose. I have to show them what she did to me."

Alrik pursed his lips. "I'm not sure that's such a good idea, Saffron. It's a long way back to the village."

"I'll be fine. I have to do this. What other proof is there? There's no bodies from the other girls, no one but two strangers and my only friend to back up the story. They need to see this."

Sam grimaced and nodded. "I think she's right," he said, looking at Mia and Alrik. "This community has been closed off from the rest of society for decades. They're not going to believe you or me, Alrik. And in their eyes, Mia will of course believe her friend."

Alrik sighed. "Ok. You're right." He turned to Saffron and said, "The quickest and safest way to take you is going to be upon my back."

Saffron swallowed the lump in her throat. "You don't mean your human back, do you?"

Alrik shook his head. "It'll be like riding Hanna, just with shaggier fur."

Saffron laughed. "Ok."

Stepping to her side, Alrik slid his muscled arms underneath Saffron's body, scooping her into his chest. With sure footed steps, he carried her outside into the small clearing outside the cabin of horrors.

"I need to put you down now. Do you think you can stand a moment?" he said.

Saffron nodded, hesitant to take her own weight on her healed leg. Holding her still injured leg up like an injured pup with a paw, Saffron tried her best to mentally block out the burning pain coming from her skinned shin. Saffron leaned against a chopped-down tree trunk for some physical support as Mia and Sam stood by her side.

Alrik smiled at Saffron and said, "You've had enough shocks for one day. I will change in the darkness of the forest."

Saffron glanced around her and nervously asked, "Um...where's the tiger?"

Alrik gave her a mischievous grin. "Roughly about halfway to China."

"You're sure? Because my dreams..." She glanced at Sam.

"I'm sure," Alrik said. "I scared him good and Sam cast a good spell on him, too." He cleared his throat and said, "Once we're moving, you can grab my fur. I run fast. You won't hurt me by doing so. If you need my attention or for me to stop, pat my head three times."

The temptation to pat his head like a dog made Saffron giggle, at least distracting her from the horrific reality of this situation. She nodded her understanding to him.

He turned from her and sprinted into the shadows, leaving her under the glaring moonlight. With all that had happened, Saffron wondered what the time was. As she debated asking Mia and Sam, who were engrossed in their own whispered conversation, the chilling howl of a wolf echoed through her body, sending shivers up and down her spine.

The ground beneath her feet vibrated. Branches snapped, and loose earth rolled across the floor. From the depths of the trees came the beast, the wolf she'd cursed and thrived off thoughts of killing for months.

He approached her with caution, watching her every muscle in case fear consumed her and took her from him again.

When he stood in front of her, his huge nose almost touching her head, she reached up to touch him, bewitched by the magnificence in front of her. He shied away from her gentle hand and lay down on his belly. Feeling almost giddy with excitement, Saffron climbed astride him, aided by Sam and Mia, and took two handfuls of his shaggy grey fur.

"How are you two getting back?" Saffron asked Mia.

Mia gave her a shy look, the flush of her cheeks visible under the lunar light. "We're not coming. We're going to wait at Alrik's cabin for you."

Saffron's heart leapt into her mouth. "You're not coming back to town?"

Mia shook her head. "I've wanted something more for years. This is my opportunity. I've made peace with this decision, Saffron. I'm ok."

"I'll heal your leg once Alrik brings you back," Sam said. "Then we'll work out our next move from there."

"What if they follow us into the forest?" Saffron asked. "Find Alrik's cabin?"

Sam shook his head. "They won't. I've hidden it with magic." His mouth twisted up into an ironic grin. "Magic similar to Adala's actually."

Saffron raised her eyebrows.

"I'm not some immortal obsessed cannibal," he replied, laughing.

Alrik turned his head and nudged Saffron's foot with the end of his nose. Saffron understood—he wanted to get going.

Giving her friend a big smile, Saffron said, "I'll see you soon."

Mia lifted her hand and waved, mirroring her friends smile. "See you real soon."

"I'm good," Saffron whispered to Alrik, revelling in this strange twist of reality.

The power with which he took off stole the breath from her body. Behind them, the ground was showered with clumps of mud from his powerful back legs. A cool breeze became an icy whip as his speed took them through the forest like they had wings. Her eyes streamed tears, and her cheeks became numb from the cold, but not once did the smile on her face falter. She felt so free and so liberated.

When her home came into view, Saffron's heart sank in disappointment.

"I don't want to go home," she whispered, tears of sadness mixing with her windswept stream. "I want to gallop through the forest forever."

Alrik faltered in his stride. Saffron jolted, falling forwards onto his withers. Upon feeling his soft coat beneath her cheek, she hummed in contentment. Talk of silver linings and clouds had always been a favourite topic of her father's. This wolf was her perfect silvery-grey lining to any cloud.

"Don't leave me," she whispered. "Please."

He nodded in response. They entered the market square from behind the town hall, and he padded straight into the centre, ignoring the screaming residents.

"He won't hurt you," Saffron shouted. "I promise. He saved me," she said, tears welling in her eyes. "I was going to kill him, and he saved me."

Alrik lay flat on his belly, waiting for Saffron to slide off him. She let go of his fur, and outstretched both of her arms around his thick neck in the best gesture of a hug she could give. Kissing him through his grey coat, she gave him her thanks and stumbled off him.

Humphrey Mayer, the lawyer, caught her before she fell. He yelled for a chair to be brought out. The September sun broke through the early morning, beaming on Saffron's pale skin, attempting to warm her icy depths. Saffron told the eerily silent crowd what had happened and finished by painfully revealing her mangled leg. Horrified gasps and shouts sounded around her as the residents put forwards their thoughts.

Saffron closed her eyes, leaned her back against the chair, and sighed, tuning out from the busy hum of excited, angry chatter around her.

It wasn't until Mr. Krüger, the owner of the bar, shouted, "So how do we rid ourselves of this curse?" that Saffron paid attention again.

Herr Fuchs stepped forwards, his hands clasped together in front of him, and replied, "The bloodline has to be cut. They *all* have to die."

CHAPTER TWENTY-FIVE

The fear that flooded Saffron at that moment surpassed any she'd felt during the night. This was an angry mob afraid for their children and their home. She knew without doubt they'd turn on her if it came down to a matter of them or her. She realised then she couldn't sympathise with them; in her world, it was her or them, and every time, she'd pick herself.

A dawning realisation of the true horrors of reality hit Saffron, making her understand that the world was still so beautiful. Regardless of where you lived, it was what you had inside you that made your life ugly or not.

Saffron glanced at Alrik. He rose and disappeared behind the town hall. When he returned, still in his glorious wolf form, he held Saffron's knife between his teeth. Smiling like crazy, she hurriedly redressed her leg. After carefully taking the knife from Alrik's mouth, she started to hobble towards the three perpetrators.

The noise around her slowly decreased until all that could be heard was her feet scuffling across the ground and the soft thud from the paws of the huge wolf alongside her. From their captive positions, tied to stakes and suspended over a metre off the ground, a trio of child-murdering cannibals stared back at her.

Adala, the infamous forest queen they'd all been taught to worship and give thanks to, stared back at her with a quirky smile tugging at her lips. Saffron stopped in front of her, turned to Alrik and whispered something into his ear.

To the witch's horror, the wolf lowered his head, allowing Saffron to sit astride his nose. He lifted her high enough to reach the woman's legs.

"What the hell are you doing?" Adala asked, almost hissing with frightened anger.

Saffron ignored her. Adala started to struggle, the creak of rope and flexing wood telling everyone of her fear. Saffron grabbed at the witch's dress and cut through the flimsy material to bare her shins.

"Well, I figured you never got to taste adrenaline-soaked flesh, so I thought I'd help you out."

Screams of protest echoed for miles, but with

Sehrstadt tucked inside the boundaries of the forest, no one could hear her except those who resided within.

Without further hesitation, Saffron leaned forwards and took the sharp blade to Adala's knee. She dug the knife in below her kneecap, blocking out Adala's painful screams. Pressing the knife into the woman's skin, Saffron ignored the nausea threatening to recoil up her throat. The healthy pink flesh gave way to the sharp blade. Blood trickled down her leg and across the knife, forever staining its purity with evil.

She forced the knife in harder and, when satisfied it was deep enough, moved her arm downwards, slicing the skin off her grandmother's shins. Upon reaching the woman's ankles, Saffron tugged at the remaining flesh holding the large flap in place. One swift slice and it was in her hands.

Alrik lifted Saffron up higher. Saffron grabbed the woman's face and dug her fingers into her cheeks to keep her mouth open.

"Fresh and warm, just for you, Grand-ma-ma."

Saffron shoved the sloppy, bloody mess into Adala's mouth. To ensure she didn't open her mouth to spit it out, Saffron placed the tip of her knife just underneath the woman's chin. After several minutes of head shakes and grunted protests, Saffron became bored.

"Swallow it," she said. "Or I'll open up your throat and stuff it down there myself."

Several seconds passed before Adala complied. "You've no idea what you've just done, you stupid little girl. You could have had all this forever. Instead you want to have a mere sixty years if you're lucky and play pat the dog."

Alrik growled, powerful vibrations coursing straight through Saffron's body. Places she never knew of ignited with excitement, catching her off guard. Her cheeks flushed red. She asked Alrik to move her to his back.

"You belong with us, Saffron," Adala said, her piercing blue eyes trying to break down Saffron's defences. "You have a taste for blood, I can see it in you. Join us. You already have blood on your hands."

Saffron looked down at her hands, smeared with Adala's blood. She looked back up at her grandmother and calmly replied, "I'm not bloodying my hands any more than necessary."

In one swift move, Alrik jumped at Adala and ripped her throat out. He then spat the mangled mess of blood and flesh at Walter.

Saffron indicated to Alrik to take her to her father. "I'm disappointed with you. How could you do this? What's wrong with you?"

Walter sneered at her, his top lip lifting back into a

snarl. "That's my mother. I would do anything for her. Clearly, you're not cut of the same cloth."

"You mean because I didn't die for you? You're sick," Saffron said, looking from her father to her mother. "Both of you are absolutely sick. Have you even thought about what's going to happen to Niklaus and the twins?"

Anna started sobbing, her chest heaving with heavy wracks of guilt. "I told you this was a bad idea, Walter, right from the start. Didn't I?"

"Shut up!" Walter shouted, glaring at his wife. He turned back to Saffron and said, "Whatever happens to your siblings is on your head, Saffron. Yours, no one else's."

Saffron smiled. "Well, I think I'll just let you die with the sweet wondering of what happened to your precious son."

Walter opened his mouth to speak but before he could utter a single word, Alrik lunged at him, ripping his throat out just like Adala's.

Anna screamed. She kicked her feet against the thick wooden pole she was tied to and tried in vain to wriggle free from her rope restraint.

"Oh, Mama, don't fret so. I'm not going to kill you."

Anna calmed down and sniffed, then smiled at her daughter. "Really?"

Saffron smiled back. "No, of course not. How could I kill my own mother?"

"I love you, Saffron," Anna said, her face beaming with hope. "I'm so sorry."

Hearing those words come from her mother's lips for the first time made Saffron feel sick. They were nothing more than words. Actions speak louder than words and her mother's actions so far had revealed nothing but a self-centred woman with her own gains in mind.

Saffron turned her back to her mother and faced the sea of faces of her community. Jerking her thumb back towards her mother, she said, "Up to you what you do with her. If anyone gets any cute ideas about immortality and sacrifices, we'll be back for you."

Anna screamed her daughter's name, begging for her to change her mind. Saffron ignored her. Whispering to Alrik it was time to go, he bounded towards the forest, taking Saffron back to his domain. All Saffron wanted now was to find her own beauty within a very fickle world.

The last that was ever seen of Saffron Schmidt was her red riding hood billowing in the wind from the back of a giant grey wolf.

## A NOTE FROM THE AUTHOR

. . .

I hope you enjoyed Saffron's story. If you did, I would be eternally grateful if you could leave a review to let others know how much you enjoyed it. Even one sentence is fine. Thank you so much!

If you want to follow me and keep up to date with all my latest goings on, visit www.cjlauthor.com and sign up for my newsletter, join my facebook group www.facebook.com/groups/lollipoplounge or look me up in the places below:

www.facebook.com/CJLaurenceAuthor
www.twitter.com/cjlauthor
www.instagram.com/cjlauthor
https://www.bookbub.com/authors/c-j-laurence

I love hearing from my readers and will always reply to you!

A NOTE FROM THE AUTHOR

I hope you enjoyed Saffron's story. If you did, I would be eternally grateful if you could leave a review to let others know how much you enjoyed it. Even one sentence is fine. Thank you so much!

If you want to follow me and keep up to date with all my latest goings on, visit www.cjlauthor.com and sign up for my newsletter, join my facebook group www.facebook.com/groups/lollipoplounge or look me up in the places below:

www.facebook.com/CJLaurenceAuthor
www.twitter.com/cjlauthor
www.instagram.com/cjlauthor
www.bookbub.com/authors/c-j-laurence

A NOTE FROM THE AUTHOR

I love hearing from my readers and will always reply to you!

ALSO BY THIS AUTHOR

Want & Need by Limitless Publishing

Cowboys & Horses

Retribution

Craving: Loyalty by Crave Publishing

Craving: One Night by Crave Publishing

Unleashing Demons

Craving: Forbidden by Crave Publishing

Unleashing Vampires

The Red Riding Hoods – The Grim Sisters Book 1

Forest of the Dark by Enchanted Anthologies

Gamechanger

Angel of the Crypt

COMING SOON:

Unleashing Werewolves

Guardians of the Temple

Who Killed Jessica James?

Snow White – The Grim Sisters Book 2

Printed in Great Britain
by Amazon